Title: Windows in the Game
Subtitle: Collection Book for Romance Short
Author: Adrienne Cotton

From the Publisher:
Thank you for purchasing this book.

Table of Contents

Title Page 1

Copyright Page 2

Bound by the Will 4

The Alien Project 63

Consumed by His Passion 106

Bound by the Will

Description

Ethan Smith is a well-known billionaire and womanizer. He doesn't believe in marriage since his mom abandoned him and his dad after he was born.

His only weakness is Jane who he sees as a sister. But, what happens when he is forced to marry Jane, his childhood best-friend. Will he still see her as a sister or as his wife?

Janelle Payne is a prominent lawyer at her father's firm. She has been in love with Ethan for years but knew he would never see her that way. Her first boyfriend ends up cheating on her, making her look pathetic. If she marries Ethan, will she fall harder for him or keep her feelings in check?

Chapter 1

Janelle clutched the pillow to her chest staring out into the darkness of her bedroom as tears rolled down her cheeks. The memories of that evening, a few hours ago played out in her mind over and over again.

***

She pulled up outside of Mike's apartment and got out of the car with a bag full of presents. She had bought him the Gucci Pour Homme fragrance, a gold Rolex wrist watch and Apple Air pods with changing case. She knew he would be pleased with the presents since he had been practically begging her for months to get them.

She knocked on the door and got no response. She knocked again still no response. She quickly checked the gift bag for her purse and fished out the spare key he had given her for emergency purposes. After a few seconds, she got the door unlocked and walked inside only to meet the house dark with no lights on. She switched on the light and sighed.

"I'm sure he's at home. I saw his car parked in the garage," she said to herself as she turned right and walked toward his bedroom.

She brought her hand up to knock on the bedroom door when she heard some muffled noises.

"Surprise! Happy Anniversa..." she began as she opened the door but paused at the scene in front of her. She closed her eyes and opened them hoping that it was just a dream.

Mike who was naked and covered up to his waist by the bedspread lay atop his co-worker, Carly. Their clothes were carelessly scattered across the room as they stared at her, the intruder.

Tense silence filled the room before Carly started to giggle.

"Finally! She knows. I was starting to wonder how long it would take for you to put two and two together."

"Shut up Carly," Mike warned as he rolled off her and sighed.

"Jane, I can explain. It's not what you think it..."

Before he could finish, she had already dashed out of the room dropping the gift bag in the process. She rushed to her car, got in and placed her head on the steering.

She felt like she was suffocating and struggling to breath with all the thoughts and questions circling her brain.

"Why am I so stupid," she asked herself repeatedly.

There was a slight knock on her window bringing her back to reality.

She looked up to see Mike standing beside her car.

"Jane, I'm sorry," he sighed as he ran his hands through his hair out of frustration, "You shouldn't have seen that."

She let out a laugh devoid of humor and rolled down the window.

"How long has this been going on?" she asked the question that had been on her mind since Carly talked earlier.

He remained silent avoiding her intense gaze. Before she could ask any further questions, Carly, now dressed in his shirt, walked up to them.

"Oh! You are still here," she giggled once again earning a glare from Mike.

"Well if you must know he didn't cheat on you. He cheated on me with you. We've been together for two years before you came into the picture. Don't ask why I allowed it. We needed your money that's all."

Jane couldn't believe her ears and turned to look at Mike for an explanation but he was looking anywhere but at her.

"He's not going to deny the truth." "Besides that, you were really stupid to think that a hot guy like Mike would be interested in a nerd like you."

***

She felt stupid, used and betrayed. She had seen the signs but she had ignored them thinking she was being paranoid, Now she wished she had paid more attention to her suspicions.

She sniffled quietly and picked up her phone, calling the one person she needed at the moment, her best friend, Ethan.

She felt her heart quicken when he picked up the phone after a few rings.

"'Hello, Jane?" he grumbled sleepily.

She felt like crying out on hearing his voice.

"Jane? Are you there?" he sounded worried.

She sniffled quietly, "Yes."

"Are you okay?"

"Why did I call him? Why?" she thought to herself.

"Jane? I'm coming over," he simply said catching her by surprise.

"No! Y-You don't have to," her voice wavered.

"Now I'm definitely coming over!" he hung up giving her no room to protest.

She slapped her forehead with her right hand feeling stupid for disturbing his sleep.

Fifteen minutes later, she heard the sound of a key being placed into the lock and the click of the lock opening.

The door opened and she heard a nervous voice call her name as he closed the door.

"Jane?"

Ethan looked around the living room for any sign of Jane. Seeing that she was not there, he rushed to her bedroom and knocked.

"It's Ethan. Can I come in?" he asked.

"Yes," she croaked. He cautiously entered and switched on the light before taking a few steps and stopping in front of her.

"Fuck, are you okay?" he asked on noticing her puffy eyes. He kicked off his shoes and climbed onto her bed in panic.

"I caught him cheating," she responded as her vision blurred with her tears.

He leaned against the headboard and pulled her to his chest while she wept against his shoulder, his arms around her as he held her close. To say he was furious was an understatement. Jane never cried but that bastard was making the tough Jane cry.

"It was our six month's anniversary and I wanted to surprise him but..." she paused "To think I almost gave myself to him."

She sounded so fragile and vulnerable, a side of Jane he had rarely seen despite being her best-friend for over twenty years. She had always put on a brave face even when her dad kept on blaming her for her mother's death. She hardly ever cried even when her dad refused to be affectionate to her. She didn't even cry when he didn't show up for her graduation.

So for him to receive a call from her at three in the morning, he knew something was wrong and it was confirmed when he heard her voice break as if she was about to cry. He didn't even think twice to drop the project he was working on and drive down to see her.

He started to stroke her hair gently with his fingertips in a bid to calm her down.

"I'm sorry. I shouldn't have disturbed your sleep," dhe apologized still feeling guilty for calling him when he should be sleeping.

"Oh! Please don't say that. I wasn't even sleeping. Besides, nothing is more important to me than you."

"Why would he do this to me, why?" she asked with a cracked voice causing his heart to ache.

He hugged her tighter and leaned his own cheek down onto the top of her head. He then began to sway with her side to side like she was a baby.

"'Because he's a jerk and a bastard. He doesn't deserve your tears."

"I feel so stupid."

"Don't be," he said, a frown on his face.

She pulled out of the hug looking anywhere else but at him.

"No, you don't understand. I was so desperate for someone to love me that I did everything for him. I turned a blind eye to the red flags thinking that I've finally found someone who loved me. But once again I was wrong. Am I that hard to love?"

He looked down at her and wondered how horrible of a friend he was not to notice her pain. He always thought she was fine but even the strong ones could break.

He had been so busy avoiding her because of that stupid will his dad made that he had turned a blind eye to Mike. He usually did a background check behind her back on all the guys who were interested in her. This one time he failed to protect her.

Mike had just messed with the wrong girl and he was going to deal with that fool in time. Right now though, all he wanted to do was stop her tears.

He cupped her face causing her to look up to meet his sad ocean blue eyes.

"Jane, don't you ever say that again. You are the most lovable person I know. Look around you. You have so many people who love you including me. Don't you ever forget all that because of a jerk."

They stared at each other for what felt like eternity.

"Thank you, Ethan," she mumbled quietly, her voice still hoarse from all the crying. She wiped her tears while he gave her a comforting smile.

"Anything for you, Jane."

He cupped her cheek again and for a split second she forgot how to breathe or the reason why she was crying in the first place.

"it's time for you to sleep," he whispered causing her heart to race at their proximity. She nodded in agreement suddenly tired from all the crying.

He made to get up but she held his hand keeping him in place while he shot her a questioning look. "Can you stay, please?" she asked shyly while he looked uncertain.

"Are you sure? I could just go sleep in the guest room."

"No I want you to stay with me. I don't want to be alone." Her eyes were pleading for him to say yes while he chuckled.

"Okay, scoot over," He stood up and turned off the light.

She felt the bed dip slightly as he climbed back into the bed and laid down facing up the ceiling.

"'Are you just going to watch me or lay down?" he asked sarcastically as he could feel her stares burning holes into him.

She smiled and laid down, resting her head on his chest while he wrapped his hands around her waist, holding her close to himself.

"Good night, Jane." he whispered.

"Good night, Ethan," she replied with a small smile and closed her eyes. It didn't take long for her to fall asleep as the crying had drained all her energy.

Chapter 2

The sound coming from the alarm slowly brought Jane back to reality. Still feeling drowsy, she reached behind her and hit snooze on the alarm before falling asleep.

After five minutes, the alarm sounded again making Jane groan loudly as she opened her eyes. She sat up slowly, feeling the hunger pangs in her tummy. She had failed to eat yesterday since she found out about her boyfriend cheating on her.

She glanced at the alarm clock and it read past seven and quickly climbed out of bed since she had to be at work at nine that morning. She rushed to the bathroom and brushed her teeth.

As she was washing her face, she looked at the mirror and blinked several times to make sure that she was staring at herself. Her brunette hair which she had kept in a loose bun was disheveled as if it had not been combed in days. Her hazel eyes were puffy with dark-purple circles under them.

"I look horrible," she muttered to herself.

Feeling downcast and hungry, she left the bathroom and took her glasses from the bedside table, wearing them in order to aid her vision.

She climbed down the stairs, making her way to the kitchen but stopped mid-way when she heard some movements. She furrowed her eyebrows trying to figure out who could be in her kitchen.

"Did Ethan leave my door open and someone broke in?" she thought to herself but shook the thoughts away, remembering that she lived in a heavily secured neighborhood.

Taking a deep breath, she pushed the kitchen door open and gasped in surprise on spotting Ethan washing her dishes.

The sound of the door opening pulled Ethan away from his deep thoughts. He turned to see Jane standing by the door, staring at him in surprise.

He placed the cup he was washing in the sink and took few steps toward her, his eyebrows furrowed in worry. "How are you feeling?"

She suddenly felt self-conscious in her leopard print pajamas under his intense gaze. It didn't help matters that she was already looking horrible.

"I'm feeling better now. I wasn't expecting that you would still be here."

He gave her a soft smile. "I left around six this morning for a change of clothes and came back."

She smiled for the first time that morning. He hadn't abandoned her even though he had a lot to do.

"Thank you," she whispered loud enough for him to hear, looking anywhere but at him. "I'm sorry I had to burden you with my problems."

"Jane'," he called gently and softly gripped her jaw to make her look at him, "you are not a burden to me. You are my best friend and I would do anything to make you happy. Anything!"

She felt her cheeks getting hotter under his intense gaze and forced a small smile wondering if he could hear the rapid beating of her heart. He stepped back a little bit and she exhaled in gratitude.

"I know you would have done the same for me." He grinned at her before turning toward the sink.

"I can't believe you are doing the dishes. Your employees would pay a fortune to see this," she chuckled as she folded her arms while watching him in amusement.

He turned back to her still grinning, "Like I said, I would do anything for you except cook because we both know I'm a terrible cook."

She laughed out loud earning a warm smile from him. He was satisfied that she was actually feeling better instead of crying over an idiot but he still wanted to make sure that she was fine.

"Are you really fine, Jane?" he asked as he narrowed his eyes at her.

The question caught her off guard that she stopped laughing. Truly, she wasn't sure how she felt but one thing she was sure of was that having Ethan there always made her feel better.

"I don't know,'" she answered truthfully meeting his sad gaze.

"I'm not as sad as I was yesterday or maybe I'm just used to getting rejected."

"Those guys are idiots."

"No, I keep on getting heart broken. So, it's obvious the problem is me. Nobody wants a nerd who dresses up like a grandma."

Anger flashed in his eyes at her statement. "Who said that to you?" he asked as gently as he could trying to control his temper.

She remained silent wishing that she had kept her mouth shut in the first place. Ethan had always been protective of her, if not over-protective. But she knew she was right this time. She was obviously the problem.

She was the nerd who always got bullied until Ethan saved her and they became friends. They had been friends since the age of ten and Ethan had always been the popular one while she was the nerd who was lucky to have him as a friend. Nobody wanted to be her friend. The girls only befriended her because of Ethan. As soon as they got his attention, they ditched her. No one even asked her out to prom. She was that pathetic but covered it up with indifference when she was actually hurting inside.

Finally, she got to meet Mike, the only guy who ever showed interest in her. Unfortunately, he was just like the rest of them.

"Was it Mike?" he asked trying to find out if the jerk was responsible.

"No, it's me."

"That's bullshit and you know that, Jane. You shouldn't let their words get to you."

She frowned suddenly offended. He would never understand her point of view. He had everything. Everyone loved him. He got away with everything while she had to work twice as hard as he did to be recognized.

"You don't understand."

"'Rhen make me understand."

"You have girls at your beck and call ready to do whatever you want them to do. I don't even have that. Not that I want that but I just want to be loved. Is that too much to ask? I didn't even get asked to the prom."

He looked pained at her words. His lips set into a tight frown as he looked directly at her, "'About prom, nobody asked you to prom because they thought you were going with me."

"What?" she asked wanting to make sure she heard him right.

"The guys thought that you were going with me. I was also surprised when I turned up at school with Melissa and everyone was asking about you."

She stared at him in disbelief, ""How? I mean was that why you left prom early to hang out with me?"

He nodded his head and put his hands in his pants pocket. He remembered that day like it was yesterday. Jane had told him that she wasn't interested in prom. Looking back now he realized she had said that so he wouldn't feel bad for her.

He had gone with Melissa, the class president who was his latest fling when people started asking him where Jane was. It was then he knew he had failed as a friend and rushed home to spend time with her watching reruns of old shows.

"And all these time I thought nobody liked me in that way," she mumbled close to tears.

He bit the inside of his lips suddenly feeling terrible. What he never disclosed to her was that he was the reason no guy had the courage to approach her in high school and college. Nobody wanted to go against the son of a multi-billionaire who owned the school. He made sure of that just because he was afraid that she would get hurt. He couldn't bear to see her heart broken.

He had been so occupied with finding a solution to his father's will that he forgot to find out more about Mike. He could have saved her but he failed to.

She forced a smile, "I have to go to work." She turned to leave but stopped in her tracks when he asked her a question.

"Are you mad at me?" he asked worried that she was pissed that he hid it from her.

She turned to look at him with an earnest expression, "I "don't care about what happened in the past. I'm just late for work and I'm sure you are too," dhe pointed out. She frowned on noticing his choice of clothes. He was dressed in a white shirt and denim jeans, the total opposite of his usual business suit.

"Why are you not dressed for work?"

"Well...I gave myself the day off and I already told your fad that you won't be reporting to work."

"And he agreed?" she asked.

"Your dad never says no to me."

He was right. Her dad adored Ethan. He was like the son he wished she was.

"But…" she protested knowing fully well that her Dad wouldn't like that.

"We're going to binge watch that Bridgerton series that you've always wanted to watch and I'm not taking no for an answer."

Her heart warmed at his kindness. She knew Ethan enough to know that he never took a break from work. He was obsessed with it and never mixed business with pleasure. So for him to cancel all that just to be with her, made her face flush and her heart swell with happiness at his kind gesture.

"Fine. I will just go take a shower."

She rushed upstairs to her room and had a quick shower.

Stepping out of the shower, she put on a black top on gray joggers and combed her hair, putting it in a neat bun. Looking into the mirror and satisfied with her appearance, she jogged downstairs excited to spend the day with Ethan.

She found him seated on the sofa a pizza box on his laps. He must have noticed her questioning look

"I ordered pizza."

She nodded while he patted the space next to him for her to sit.

They spent the next hour discussing the movie and fighting over the last piece of pizza like they always do.

He used the remote to reduce the volume and looked down at the sleeping beauty whose head was resting on his shoulder. She had dozed off in the middle of the movie.

She stirred from sleep and opened her eyes only to meet his.

"Marry me, Jane." he whispered loud enough for her to hear.

She blinked several times before sitting up and staring at him "What did you say?"

"I asked you to marry me."

Her eyes widened in surprise. She hadn't been dreaming after all. She burst out laughing but stopped when he didn't join in.

"You are joking, right?"

"I'm serious." He maintained eye contact staring at her seriously.

She frowned confused.

I must be dreaming. It can't be true but he looks so serious, she thought to herself.

Seeing the conflicted look on her face, he placed his hand on hers.

"I know you're confused but I think it's the best solution to our problems. You need to be noticed and respected and you can get that by being my wife."

She released her hand from his "I don't...what are you talking about?"

"Remember I told you my dad's will stated that I would only be able to inherit his properties if I get married."

She nodded. She knew that he had disclosed that to her before. She just didn't understand what it had to do with her.

He rubbed the back of his neck "He actually named the woman he wanted me to marry and it's you."

She stared at him in disbelief waiting for him to burst out in laughter and tell her it was all a joke but he was staring at her seriously.

"It's you, Jane. He wants me to marry you"

"Why? Why me?"

"Exactly, he knows that I see you as the little sister I never had. Imagine my surprise when the news came out."

"Why are you just telling me this now?"

"You were in a relationship. I didn't want to disrupt your happiness."

"I can't believe this. Why me?"

He sighed. "Thinking about it now, my dad made the right choice. I'm sure he knew I was just going to pay a random girl to be my wife."

"This is too much."

He turned to her, holding her two hands in his while staring at her intensely. "Look at the bright side, when you get married to me no one is going to disrespect you."

"What are people going to think. Nobody would believe this."

"Everyone I know wants us together no matter how ridiculous it is."

"Still," she protested.

"Jane, it's all up to you."

"But I thought you said you've found a way out."

"I only said that because I didn't want to worry you."

"Am I the only one who knows about this?" she asked.

He shook his head.

"Ryan and your dad knows but they didn't tell you because I told them not to."

She stood up and started pacing trying to process the information.

"We're just going to stay married for a year and six months to make it believable," he said trying to make her see reason. He wasn't planning on breaking the news to her that way especially when she was still upset with catching Mike cheating on her. It just kind of came out and he couldn't stop himself.

She stopped pacing and looked down at him. "That doesn't help matters. I don't want to be a divorcee especially after one year of marriage. I'm already called so many awful names, I don't want to add another."

He stood up and placed his hands on her shoulder. "Jane, you have a lot to gain than lose in this. Everyone would have no choice but to respect you and that your foolish ex would realize what a fool he was to let you go."

She turned away from him while he sighed and brushed his hair back.

"Jane, I don't believe in marriage. At the same time I don't want this but my hands are tied. I'm about to lose the company I worked so hard to revive just because my dad doesn't want me to be alone in this world."

He paused trying to calm down and then continued, "If I had a choice you wouldn't even know about this. Whatever your decision is, I will respect it."

She still didn't turn to look at him, her arms folded as she tried to make sense of the situation.

"I hate myself for putting you in this uncomfortable situation so I'm just going to leave," he stated and picked up his phone and walked out leaving her to her thoughts.

Chapter 3

To say Ethan was nervous was an understatement. He was freaking out and trying really hard not to pace back and forth because of the press. There were a few of them which he had approved to cover the wedding.

He took a glance at his wrist watch for the hundredth time that morning and cursed.

Ryan who had been watching amusedly at his friend placed a hand on his shoulder to calm him down. " It's only been five minutes, she'll be her soon," he assured Ethan.

"What if, she changed her mind at the last minute?" he voiced out his concern.

Ryan rolled his eyes. "You know more than anyone that Jane would never disappoint you."

Ethan nodded. He knew Ryan was right. Jane would never do anything to hurt him and he loved her for that. It was two weeks after he told her about the will that she agreed to marry him and he didn't waste any time in preparing for the wedding. Since he only had five months left to fulfil his father's wishes.

His thoughts were cut short when the press turned their camera to the entrance. Mr. Payne came in with Jane holding on to his arm. Ethan felt his mouth go dry on seeing her dress. It was a white silk V-neck jumpsuit which hugged her body just right, showcasing her hourglass shape. Her makeup was simple save for a nude lipstick which made her luscious lips stand out more. She looked amazing. He didn't know how long he had been staring at her until Ryan nudged him with a knowing look.

He cleared his throat and fixed his black suit. Mr. Payne acknowledged him with a nod while he handed over Jane to him.

"Hi," he greeted her as he led her to the front stage. She smiled back not meeting his eye making him more nervous.

"Did I do something wrong?" he asked.

Before Jane could offer an explanation, the judge had already started with the introduction but that didn't stop Ethan from staring at her.

Her dad had been nice to her that day. Telling her how proud he was that she was marrying Ethan. She wondered why he even kept quiet about the will when he was the lawyer who made it and clearly wanted her to end up with Ethan.

"Do you, Janelle Payne, take Ethan Smith as your lawfully wedded husband to have and to hold from this day forward, for better, for worse, for richer, for poorer, in sickness and in health until death do us part?"

She could feel everyone's eyes on her but she couldn't bring herself to say anything. She met Ethan's confused gaze and almost felt like crying.

"Why am I doing this again?" she asked herself. She was too young to get married after all she was only twenty-seven.

She knew she was about to sign a year and six months of her life to Ethan, the man she had loved for sixteen years and that scared her to the brim. She didn't know whether she could survive being with him without hoping and getting hurt at the same time because he would never see her that way.

However, she remembered the promise she had made to his father on his sick bed that she would take care of Ethan. Back then he had insisted that she would understand in time. Even though she still didn't understand his motive, she would not dare break the promise and her friend's trust in the process. So she gathered all her wit and faced the wedding officiate.

"Yes, I do."

The wedding officiate sighed in relief and turned to look at Ethan who still seemed to be shaken by the suspense.

"Do you Ethan Smith , take Janelle Payne as your lawfully wedded wife to have and to hold from this day forward, for better, for worse, for richer, for poorer, in sickness and in health until death do us part?"

"I do." He wasted no time answering wanting to get it over and done with.

They were told to exchange rings which they did while Jane was still avoiding his gaze making him worried.

"By the power vested in me, I now pronounce you husband and wife. You may now kiss the bride." the wedding officiate announced with a smile.

They both froze with Jane finally looking up to meet Ethan's shocked gaze. They hadn't discussed this. In fact they didn't plan on doing that.

He came closer, his eyes burning holes into her making her nervous. He lifted her chin and snaked his arms around her waist pulling her close.

She gasped at their closeness, her heart beating frantically against her chest as she wondered what his next move would be.

"Trust me," he whispered and leaned in. They were only inches away from each other's face when his eyes flicked down to her lips and he swallowed nervously.

He planted his lips against hers and she froze, heat spreading across her body like a wildfire. Her lips were soft and felt like home. Before he could control himself, he sucked on her bottom lip asking for entrance. She let out a moan and he took the opportunity and explored the wet cavern of her mouth. She felt high and confused as he deepened the kiss.

The sound of clapping from the guests made them pull apart so fast it felt like a dream.

The realization of what just happened hit him as they signed their marriage license. He had planned on pecking her lips but ended up doing the exact opposite. He couldn't even look at her without feeling guilty for breaking her trust. It certainly didn't help matters that he wanted to do it again.

If no one was there, he would have continued kissing her so much that he feared he wouldn't have been able to stop himself. He felt disgusted thinking about her like that when she was clearly uncomfortable.

He was still thinking of how he could escape the uncomfortable situation when the press bombarded him with questions and congratulations making him feel thankful for the distraction.

"How was it?" Ryan teasingly asked a flustered Jane who had been looking at her feet since the kiss.

"How was what?" She glared at him despite her flustered state while he raised his arms in surrender.

"The kiss, what else would I be talking about?" Ryan rolled his eyes convinced that she was playing ignorant on purpose.

She didn't have an answer for that. She truly was still trying to recover from the shock of having her best friend kiss her.

"You know I really wasn't expecting you guys to make out in front of the press," Ryan stated.

She sighed and nodded, "I wasn't expecting it either."

They hadn't drawn up a contract yet because Ethan was in a hurry to get them married as soon as possible. However, they had agreed that there would be no physical intimacy between them which had now been broken by Ethan.

Ethan found himself staring at Jane from across the room trying to gauge her reaction. If he wasn't her best-friend, he would think that she was perfectly ok but he knew her enough to know that she was asking herself a lot of questions. He decided that he just couldn't avoid her all day without making things awkward.

He finally excused himself from the press and made his way toward her and Ryan. He signaled to Ryan to give them some privacy, unbeknownst to Jane who was looking at her feet.

Scenting Ethan's cologne, she looked up to meet his piercing ocean eyes.

"Janelle, I'm sorry about the kiss. I shouldn't have done that but I didn't have a choice because of the media being present."

She felt her heart break at his words but forced a smile "You don't have to apologize. I already prepared for this," she lied.

Ethan had kissed her for the press. This was going to be on the news the next day which would make their marriage more believable. That was why he did it and not for any other reason. She felt stupid thinking that maybe it meant something to him when it clearly didn't.

"I already made sure that the press wouldn't bother you and answered questions on your behalf."

He scanned the registry for a few seconds before turning his attention back to her "It's time to go home so just smile and hold on to my arm as I lead you outside to the car."

She nodded and obeyed with the cameras zooming in on them as they left the registry.

She exhaled in relief on entering the car after feeling overwhelmed with the cameras.

"Are you okay?" Ethan asked in concern.

She was startled out of her thoughts by his question and looked up only to see him leaning toward her. Her eyes widened at the proximity and blushed hard as she suddenly remembered the kiss they shared a few minutes ago.

She nodded and shifted putting a little space between them on the pretense of adjusting her dress so that he wouldn't be suspicious.

He narrowed his eyes at her not buying for a second that she was okay but decided to let it go. He turned to face the road and starting the car and drove away.

The silence in the car was suffocating him and he couldn't help but think that he was at fault for making things awkward between them by kissing her. He cleared his throat gaining her attention.

"I didn't allow Bill to drive because I wanted us to have some privacy." He started taking a quick glance at her before focusing on the road as he drove.

"Privacy for what?" she asked confused, her eyes on him.

He gave her the file he had taken from his seat when he first entered the car.

"For the contract I kept on postponing due to me adding and re-adding some clauses."

She pulled out the papers and started reading through while he placed his free hand on hers stopping her from reading, his eyes still focused on the road as he drove.

"You don't have to read that now. It's just for formality sake. I just wrote what we agreed upon. We could have affairs as long as they sign an NDA and we would make appearances together when necessary. The only physical touching allowed is hugging..."

He paused and chuckled nervously, "I already broke that one."

"I'll have to draw up another contract because what happened today made me realize that maybe us kissing wouldn't be so bad."

Jane felt her heart take a crazy leap as she frowned trying to make sense of his words.

He must be joking, she thought but there was nothing on his face which gave that away.

She cleared her throat and asked, "What made you come to that conclusion?"

"I just realized that we didn't think this through. Nobody is going to believe that this is a real marriage if all we do is hug each other like we usually do as best friends. It would make things more believable if we shared a kiss when necessary."

His hand gripped the steering wheel unconsciously, as he couldn't believe that he was making that suggestion to his best friend. However, he couldn't help it. He wanted to feel those soft lips on his again and how high he felt when he kissed them. He would do anything just to taste those luscious lips of hers again just to get those feelings back.

She laughed out loud trying to hide how giddy she felt. "You are joking, right?"

"Does it look like I am?"

She gasped and looked at him in surprise wondering if she was dreaming. He had just apologized to her a while ago as if he was repulsed by the fact that they kissed and now the guy who happened to be her best friend in the whole world and who was way out of her league was asking for a kiss.

"Here we are," he announced as he pulled the car to a stop in front of the magnificent gate of his mansion. The gate opened and he drove in and parked in the garage.

She slowly got of the car and closed the door behind her.

" Are you not coming inside?" she asked in concern when she saw that he made no move to come out of the car.

"Yeah, I have some work to do at the office. I'll be back before ten o'clock tonight," he lied. He just needed some time alone to understand why he wanted to kiss her again.

He attributed it to the fact that he needed to get laid which was why he was having these weird feelings and in order not to jeopardize their friendship, he needed to leave as soon as possible before he compromised her or did something that she wouldn't be able to forgive him for.

That night she waited for him but he didn't come home and the night after that.

Chapter 4

"What about this?" Jane asked as she stood in front of Ryan displaying the black gown she wore. She was at Ryan's house trying on the clothes she had bought from the boutique.

Ryan looked up in time and frowned "Oh! God. it's a no."

"This is the third time you rejected what I picked," Jane said annoyed that Ryan had always found something wrong with her dress choices.

"Yeah that's because, I don't see any difference. You need dresses Jane not black mourning gowns.

She sighed and sat next to him on the bed. She was already exhausted. Ryan had called her a few hours ago to inform her that she and Ethan were going to a business dinner.

To say she was amazed was an understatement. Ethan hadn't bothered to call her, neither had she seen him for two weeks since their wedding. It was like he was avoiding her and she didn't know what she had done wrong to deserve it. Ryan was his spoke person who tried to alleviate her worry that Ethan was just busy but she knew better.

"I'm sorry okay. I was just trying to help."

"Well, you're not helping. You keep on typing on your phone instead of helping me pick dresses and when I pick one, you dislike it. Weren't you the one who said I should change my look in the first place?"

He sat up and said, "Yeah I was the one. Have you forgotten how beautiful you looked in that jumpsuit I chose for your wedding? "

"You know what, this is a bad idea." She made to stand up but he pulled her back down.

"No, it's not. You signed up for this. What would everyone think if you didn't attend this dinner with him as his wife? It would create gossip and make everyone doubt your relationship."

"Besides, everyone will be interested in you and your background which is why you have to put more efforts in your outfits."

She sighed knowing that he was telling the truth but that didn't make her feel any better.

"So I'm only needed when he needs to make an appearance and he will disappear soon after, leaving me in the dark," she stated bitterly.

He placed his hand on your shoulder, squeezing it reassuringly. "We both know this marriage is nothing but a joke to him but it means so much to you because you love him."

She looked at her hands suddenly finding interest in her fingers. Ethan had met Ryan in college and introduced him to her. Since then they had been as thick as thieves. He knew more than anyone that she had feelings for Ethan.

"You know sometimes I stare at him and I'm amazed at how much of a fool not noticing you. Like, it's so disheartening but at the same time I warned you about this. Will your heart be okay doing this?"

That was a question she didn't have an answer to. She had thought about Ethan's offer of marriage over and over before accepting it. She had thought that she would be indifferent and would be able to keep her feelings in check but she was so wrong. The fact that he was avoiding her after their kiss only showed her that he would never love her that way and that broke her heart.

Seeing her faraway look and not wanting to make her sad, he decided to change the subject,

"You know what, I bought some dresses for you before you came over."

He called his help over and whispered something into her ear while Jane looked on confused.

"What are you doing."

"Just wait and see," he said as he winked at her while the help left.

The help came back a few minutes later with a rack full of gowns of different colors and lengths.

"I'm not wearing those." She shook her head as she stared at the rack in wonder.

"You are. In fact you must."

"Whydo I have to wear these?"

" You signed up for this. Just think of it as a wedding gift"

Just then Ethan walked in, dressed to the nines in his expensive dark blue suit.

"Hi guys," he greeted them with a smile.

"What's going on here and why are you looking so downcast," he asked as he stared at Jane who had a forlorn look on her face.

"Ah! Thank God you're here. Please help tell Jane that she needs to change her look."

Ethan frowned, his hands in his pocket as he looked confusedly at Ryan. "Why does she need to? She's okay the way she is."

Ryan face palmed himself and sighed. "You know how vicious the media can be. This is going down in history. We have to make an effort to make it believable."

"Fine, I will change," Jane declared and picked up a dress before heading for the bathroom to change. Anything to get away from Ethan.

"She didn't even look at me or acknowledge my presence," Ethan muttered under his breath but loud enough for Ryan to hear.

Ryan rolled his eyes at his friend's foolishness. "Yeah Duh! What kind of a man leaves his wife hanging for two weeks after their wedding? Did you really expect her to hug you after ghosting her?”

“Yeah ,you’re right.”

“I’m always right,” Ryan maintained, “But seriously, why did you leave Jane hanging like that. She didn’t deserve that. You made her think that she did something wrong. What is wrong with you, man?

How could he tell Ryan that he was running away from his confusing feelings for Jane? He had gone years seeing her as a sister and nothing else until the kiss happened and unlocked something in him.

How could he tell him that he needed some time away to process his emotions and find out why he wanted so badly to push her against the wall and kiss her senseless.

Jane stepped into the room dressed in a dark blue straps V-neck side slit floor length dress and stood in front of Ryan showcasing her dress.

Ryan eyes widened as he stared at her dress before standing up and smiling widely. “My God! This is it. It looks so good on you,” he commented.

“If I weren’t gay, I would never let you slip away.”

“What do you think, Ethan?” Ryan asked Ethan.

Jane glanced at Ethan who seemed to be scanning her dress, his eyes held a mystery which made her anxious.

The dress hugged her curves in the right places making him light-headed. He had never wanted to bed a woman as much as he did right now. He yearned to bury himself inside her for hours and give into the pleasure he had denied himself for so long.

He had never felt this way about a woman before and the fact that he was feeling this way for Jane, his best friend, scared him more than anything.

"I don't like it. It's too revealing," he said for his own sanity. He couldn't be by her side all night in that dress. She was going to be the death of him.

Anger flashed in her eyes at his audacity. "I'm wearing this dress whether you like it or not." Even though she wasn't comfortable in the dress, she wouldn't allow Ethan to boss her around especially not after he abandoned her.

Ryan raised his eyebrow at him as if saying, "what is wrong with you?"

"Suit yourself." He buried his hands in his pocket and glared at her "Meet me downstairs when you are done." With that being said, he walked out.

Chapter 5

She hadn't said a word to him since they arrived at the party, although he should be thankful for that. Her silence was driving him crazy and it didn't help matters that all eyes were on them especially on Jane who looked absolutely beautiful.

He was trying really hard not to gawk at her in that dress.

"Look who we have here, my favorite man Ethan Philips," Ben Pratt said as he walked up to Ethan and Jane.

Ethan smiled on noticing his company's loyal customer, Ben, and they shared a quick hug while Ben eyes were focused on Jane who wanted to be anywhere but there at that moment.

"Is she ...your wife?" he turned to look at Ethan who nodded. "I mean I saw it on the news but I had a hard time believing that the chronic womanizer had gotten married."

He smiled at Jane. "But now I can see why you decided to settle down. She's such a pretty young lady."

"Hi, I'm Ben...Ben Pratt and you are?" he introduced himself as he shook her hands marveling at how soft her hands were.

"Janelle Pay...Smith." She quickly corrected herself smiling nervously.

"I must say Ethan got himself a priceless jewel."

She forced a smile not really pleased with the way he was looking at her.

Ethan cleared his throat catching Ben's attention. "What brings you here?" he asked trying to hide his annoyance.

Ben chuckled finally looking at Ethan. "Jaden Macauley is here and he wants to speak with you."

Ethan eyes lit up at the information. Jaden Macauley was the biggest billionaire America ever produced and he also happened to be his role model. He had always wanted to meet him and here he was.

"Come, I'll take you to him. You can thank me later." Ben offered while Ethan looked back at Jane, reluctant to leave her alone all to herself. However, she smiled at him encouraging him to go. He sighed and followed Ben.

It had been ten minutes since Ethan had left and she was bored. She didn't like being the center of attraction especially with the men eyeing her and the woman giving her the side eye. She wished she had listened to Ethan and just picked a dress she was comfortable in.

A woman stood a few feet away from her catching her attention. She wore a white see through lace gown which left little to the imagination. Her blonde hair was packed up in a bun, with two strings of hair falling over her face. She took a sip out of her wine glass while scanning Jane's dress with distaste.

"Ethan really disappointed me, you know."

Jane raised her eyebrow in question wondering why the gorgeous woman was talking to her.

"When he told me he had gotten married, I expected better not a low life like you."

"Excuse me?" Jane frowned surprised by the insult.

The woman threw her head back chuckling. "He told me everything about this sham of a marriage. He was with me the night of your wedding. We made sweet love and he was screaming my name all night. But don't worry I won't tell anyone."

Jane eyes widened as she took in the information. She felt like she had just been kicked in the stomach. She scanned the room for Ethan and spotted him happily chatting with Jaden Macauley.

So he couldn't even honor our wedding night, she thought sadly.

Jane had a few words for the stupid woman in front of her but she held back deciding not to give her the pleasure of knowing she got under her skin. She forced a smile and walked away looking for the waiter in need for a drink.

She was about to down her second glass of vodka when it was snatched away by Ben.

"Nah I can't let you get drunk." He downed the vodka on her behalf.

"How is that any of your business?" she snapped. Everyone seemed to be dictating how she should live her life while they had fun forbidding her to the same.

"With the way you were burning holes into Ethan from across the room, I would say he did you wrong." He gave her a knowing look.

"I wouldn't blame you though what kind of a husband would leave his wife alone."

"Your Point?"

"My point is, you deserve better than him. He can't stay faithful to you neither can he respect you. You need a capable and loving man."

"What is going on here?" Ethan asked as he approached them. He had been engrossed in his chat with Mr. Macauley until he noticed Ben's disappearance. He didn't think twice to know that he would be flirting with Jane.

"Just keeping your wife company since you abandoned her."

"I think your work is done here, you can leave now!"

"I think we should let her decide that." Ben turned to look at Jane who rolled her eyes yearning to leave the party.

She made to leave but Ethan held her back making her glare at him "Let me go," she said as she tried to get out of his grip but he was too strong for her.

"We came together. We leave together," he said with an air of finality.

"Don't you think it would be better if you leave with one of your conquest here. Since that's what you are good at," Jane said.

He frowned confused. "What are you talking about?"

Ben chuckled. " You are really naïve."

Ethan glared at Ben who lifted his hands in surrender and walked away knowing better than to provoke him any further.

"Let me go," she said as she tried to wriggle out of his grip on her hand.

"Don't cause a scene," he warned.

"Of course, all you care about is your damn reputation."

Ethan regarded Jane for a moment before releasing her hand and following her out of the party.

"What are you talking about?" he asked. He didn't know what he had done to make her so angry.

She didn't answer him. Instead she kept on walking until she reached the car.

"Jane I'm talking to you." He was slowly losing his temper by her attitude.

She turned to look at him. "Would you like to talk here especially when everyone is looking at us."

She was right. There were guests outside having a drink or two and they were starting to stare at them.

They got into the car while Bill, his driver, drove the car.

Throughout the ride home, she was just looking outside the window ignoring him as if he wasn't there. He wanted so badly to ask her questions and put this behind them but he couldn't do it with Bill present so he just kept his mouth shut until they entered the house.

"Look Jane, I'm sorry that I left you alone. That was so cruel of me," he apologized as he closed the front door behind him.

She let out a laugh devoid of humor shaking her head at him. "You disgust me."

"What? What did I do?" he was genuinely confused.

She rolled her eyes. "Oh! Please. You know what I'm talking about. You left me hanging in the dark for two weeks. Two weeks! You didn't even call or text me. I was worried sick about you only for you to call Ryan and tell him that you were okay."

She paused taking a deep breath then continued "Then I decided to put my anger aside and follow you to that party. Guess who came to meet me?" she asked moving closer to him, her hazel eyes piercing his.

He remained silent knowing better than to interrupt her when she was venting.

"Your mistress! You told her about this marriage being a sham when we both agreed that nobody else apart from Ryan would know about this. I was worried sick all this time but you were somewhere fucking your mistress." She yelled the last part causing him to take a step back. He had never seen her, this angry, ever.

He already knew who she was referring to. It was Clara a top model one of his many flings. He had called her over that night to get laid and clear his head from his improper thoughts about Jane. However, he failed miserably because nothing happened between them to his dismay.

"Nothing happened between me and Clara okay," he clarified "I may have told her the truth when I was drunk but nothing happened.'"

"I don't care!" she yelled.

"Then why are you so angry?" he yelled back.

"I'm angry because my 'so called best friend' left me hanging with no explanation at all. I deserve an explanation!"

He closed the space between them, their nose almost touching. To say that she was intimidated was an understatement, she took a step back but before she could move away any further, he held unto her free hand and pulled her toward him making her collide with his chest.

"What are you doing?" she managed to ask.

He smiled. "What I should have done a long time ago."

Before she could digest his words, he leaned in and touched his lip with hers, the second he touched her soft plump lips he lost himself to the hunger inside him and pushed his tongue past her lips to swim the depths of her mouth. A soft sigh escaped her throat before her tongue twined with his exploring his mouth as he did hers. It only takes her few seconds to realize that she was kissing her best friend whom she was supposed to be furious with. She gathered all her strength and pushed him away.

He sighed and brushed his hair back in frustration. "I want you so much it hurts and I'm not going to apologize because I'm not sorry. That's why I left because I can't keep my hands to myself when I'm with you."

Her body tingled under his sinfully dark gaze. She couldn't believe her ears. Her mind was in disarray at his confession. She should be jumping for joy because he wanted her but she just stood there more confused than ever.

He caressed her cheeks causing tingles on her body. "Tell me to stop."

Jane wasted no time in wrapping her hands on the back of his neck and capturing his lips with a searing kiss. He took over by kissing her back hungrily and before she knew it, he had reached down and lifted her up by the hips, her back resting against the wall with her legs wrapped around his waist.

She nearly whined when he broke the kiss. His eyes searched hers looking for any form of regret but he smiled when he only saw lust. He kissed her again carrying her easily as he turned and slowed down. He broke the kiss for a second to open the door and when they entered she realized they were in the guestroom.

Placing her down gently so her feet connected to the floor, they both kicked off their shoes as he walked her backward toward the bed.

Laying her down gently on the bed, he crawled between her parted legs. He connected his lips to hers more urgently this time. He gave her lower lip a gentle suck, then a nibble asking for permission which she immediately granted.

He moved to her neck mapping every inch with kisses and bites leaving his marks. He continued to trail a line of kisses under her collarbone, up her neck. By now she was a moaning mess so lost in her pleasure that she didn't notice when he stripped her clothes off leaving her completely naked before his hungry eyes.

"You are beautiful, Janelle," he whispered.

He went straight to cup her left breast, licking a strip over the most sensitive part. He sucked on it gently making her head fall back into a mass of pillows, back aching in impossible pleasure.

"Fuck!" she moaned lowly.

He gave it a hard suck before moving to the next mound repeating the same action.

He trailed kisses down her stomach making her squirm. His fingers made a shallow deep rubbing over her mound which made her eyes roll back and her entire body squirm.

She moaned loudly biting her lip to stop herself from screaming. His fingers retreated and she sighed in both relief and disappointment but it didn't last long.

Before she could control her breathing, he was down between her legs as she felt a warm breeze on her core. He began to flick his tongue sucking and circling making her yelp.

"Oh my God! Ethan," she cried out.

He began to pick up the pace, his fingers dipping in and out of her quickly. Her hand gripped his hair so hard she feared she might have ripped some of it. One second she was moaning for more, the next she was crying and begging him to stop.

She opened her eyes to meet his darkened eyes, giving off a hunger she knew her eyes also reflected. She watched him slowly unzip his trousers and with one pull, it fell to the ground in a heap. Her eyes zeroed on the bulge through his black boxers an ache spreading between her legs.

Suddenly afraid at how huge he was, she confessed, "Ethan...ï...I have never done this before."

"Not even with Mike?" he asked in disbelief.

She shook her head. To say he was shocked was an understatement. The right thing to do now was to stop this and pretend it never happened but he couldn't. It was too late, he was down too deep. No one had ever aroused him that much.

He took off his top revealing his toned stomach and pulled his boxers down.

He leaned over her on the bed and swept her mouth with his tongue. "I promise to be gentle."

She nodded bracing herself. She desperately desired him even though she was nervous.

Wasting no time, he settled between her thighs again aligning himself with her. He pushed in gently, inch by inch, to slowly allow her to adjust until he was completely seated. He then caught her whimpers with a deep kiss.

He let her breathe for a second before he slowly started to pick up pace. He leaned up on his arms thrusting into her faster and faster while her fingers wrapped around his muscular back gripping on for dear life as moans and groans filled the room.

He changed the angle by pushing her legs higher around his waist. He began to thrust even harder and quicker making her scream in pleasure, nails digging his back. "Oh, God, Ethan. Ethan...aah...aah."

His eyes locked unto hers as their bodies connected. One hand was on the back of his neck, the other under his arm, clawing at his back.

His eyes were locked unto hers, studying her every reaction.

Feeling her tighten around him, he increased his pace as he pursued his own release.

"Just let go."

As if it was the magic word, her feet curled and her body arched. Jane screamed her orgasm yelling his name.

His real undoing was watching her orgasm as he soon found release groaning her name.

Ragged moans left his parted lips as they let each other ride their pleasures until the end. With one last thrust, he stilled inside her

"Wow!" he exclaimed.

He slowly pulled out of her still sensitive body in a bid not to crush her and dropped next to her. They laid there catching their breath.

He stood up and left for the bathroom.

A few seconds later he came back with a warm towel and started to wipe the blood between her legs. It took every will power in him not to take her again. He disposed of the towel and climbed in bed with her.

She could feel herself being pulled to sleep when she felt him wrap his arms around her before pulling the covers over them.

The last thing she felt was him placing a gentle kiss on her neck before she fell into the best sleep she had ever had.

Chapter 6

Sunlight invaded the bedroom through the large windows hitting his face. He frowned and squinted his eyes to adjust to the light.

He laid there for a few seconds confused on why he was not in his room. He then became aware of the weight on his arm and the constant airy tickle at the back of his neck.

His heart skipped a bit as the memories of last night replayed in his head. He had actually had sex with Jane, his best friend.

"Shit," he grunted quietly.

As he stared at the sleeping girl next to him, his heart sank with the fact that he had taken her virginity. An honor he didn't deserve. He had had plenty of sex in his life time but they all faded in comparison to last night.

He slowly removed his arm from underneath her sleeping frame and climbed out of bed as quietly as possible.

He carefully picked up his boxers and shirt and put them on. He eyed her sleeping figure one last time before he slipped out.

He needed to get out of there as soon as possible. She deserved better than him. Last night had already established that she wanted him as much as he wanted her and although that pleased him. Those new found feelings scared him. He couldn't afford to let his demons consume her.

The thought of wanting to be with her forever, haunted him because he knew what it implied but he was not ready for that. He doubted that he would ever be.

He had commitment issues. If he had been afraid of getting hurt before, now he was afraid that he would be the one to hurt her.

He had watched how his dad pined after his mom even after she abandoned him for another man. He never recovered and that had no doubt contributed to his illness which later led to his death six months ago.

After watching his dad wallow in self-pity, he had vowed to never let a woman capture his heart. Jane had been the only constant woman in his life and now he had ruined that by being intimate with her.

He needed a cold shower. He rushed to his bathroom and stayed in the shower for ten minutes before stepping out and sighing.

Ten minutes later, he climbed down the stairs now dressed in a dark blue pressed suit.

Desperately in need of a drink, he went to the bar and brought out a bottle of whiskey. He popped it open and downed the content not bothering to pour it into a cup. He placed the bottle on the bar table and exhaled. He never drank in the morning especially when he had to be at work in a few minutes time but the events of last night called for something strong to deal with it.

His thoughts were interrupted when he heard someone approaching. He looked up in time to see Jane approaching him.

He swallowed hard as his eyes trailed down her night robe dying to feel her under him again.

She had a glint in her eye as she smiled at him. "I thought you left me alone." She had woken up a few minutes ago looking for Ethan thinking that maybe he regretted what happened between them. Now she was relieved that he didn't leave her like an insignificant one night stand.

She could feel the awkwardness in the air as Ethan nervously looked anywhere but her.

Call her naive but she needed to know where they stood. She didn't regret last night. She was happy that it was the man she loved that she slept with.

Hating the silence she cleared her throat catching his attention. "Ethan, can we talk?"

He froze and licked his lips nervously. "If this is about what happened last night, forget it."

Her heart sank "Why?"

He looked down at the bottle suddenly finding interest in its content ."Last night was a mistake. It shouldn't have happened. I'm sorry."

She felt her lungs tighten as she winced at his words.

"It didn't mean anything to you?" she said to herself but he heard her.

"Yes, it was just sex, nothing else." He felt like a jerk breaking her heart like that. He had never been cruel to a woman even his flings but the one woman he cared about, he was treating her like trash.

She could feel herself wanting to cry but she would be damned if she did so in front of him. She took a few deep breaths to keep herself calm and slapped herself mentally for being so stupid. She should have seen it coming but she had let her hopes take over and now she was paying the price.

"It meant a lot to me because I gave myself to the man I love and I don't regret it."

He stood up from his seat "You love me?" He couldn't have heard her correctly.

She rolled her eyes at his stupidity. "I've always loved you. I was there when you moved from all the Melissas and Kims in town. I was in the side lines hoping that one day you would see me and I thought that last night meant something to you but I thought wrong."

"What the hell!" he muttered under his breath.

She had always loved him and now he had broken her heart beyond repair. To think he was initially worried that he had lost her friendship but alas, he had done worse.

He ran his fingers through his hair and bit his lips hating himself for what he was about to say next. "Is that why your dad manipulated my dad into forcing me to marry you? You just couldn't stay in the side lines any longer and took advantage of my vulnerability last night."

She slapped him hard on his cheek causing him to gasp in surprise. He knew he deserved it. He deserved worse from her.

"Fuck you, Ethan. I can't believe this is you." The tears she had been trying to prevent, rolled down her cheeks as her voice broke.

"Well you better believe it. Did you really think you could change me just because of a one night stand?" he scoffed "You are really naive."

"It was just sex. It meant nothing to me so the sooner you get over it, the better for the two of us," he snapped.

She shook her head as she stared at him with tear stricken eyes. He didn't look or sound like the man she loves. He was different. The total opposite of the caring Ethan she had always known. If she knew that sleeping with him would unleash the devil in him, she would have stopped last night from happening.

She wiped her tears and forced a smile. "Fine. It's totally fine."

She looked away and sniffed. "I'm not going to stand here and be disrespected while pretending that everything is fine. My job here is done. You've gotten your inheritance, there's no need for any more pretense."

"Don't worry, we'll stay married as stipulated in the contrac,t but I'm not going to live here anymore nor am I going to go out on dates with you pretending that we're a happy couple."

She quickly turned away headed for her room to pack her stuffs. She muttered a sorry to Ethan's father. She couldn't do this anymore. She just couldn't.

He fell down to his knee, his heart pounded against his chest as he started to tremble. He didn't mean any of what he said. He wanted so badly to beg her not to leave, to tell her that he would change for her. It hurt him to hurt her like that but he was a lost case. She couldn't fix him, no one could.

She climbed down the stairs dragging her luggage with her. She spotted him on the floor and almost rushed to ask if he was okay but she stopped herself. She couldn't be a fool anymore and run to him every time like a lap dog. He didn't need her, he never needed her.

She walked past him to the door and gave him one last look "Goodbye Ethan". and banged the door after her.

Her words were cold and distant and the finality behind them hit him hard.

"Goodbye Ethan." It kept on ringing in his ear.

"This is what you wanted so why does it feel like my heart is being ripped out off my chest." he asked himself.

He knew the answer to that. If he had been ignoring his feelings before, there was no point now. He couldn't deny it anymore. He was in love with her totally and completely.

Chapter 7

Jane pushed the strand of hair that had been disturbing her vision behind her ear as she studied the file before her. It contained the facts of the divorce case she was in charge of. The couple had cited irreconcilable differences as grounds for their divorce and it made her think of Ethan.

She hadn't seen or talked to him in two months and it was driving her crazy. She wished he would just walk in and apologize and they could go back to being friends at least but that was all wishful thinking. The mere fact that he didn't bother to contact her convinced her the more that he was done with her.

Her stomach grumbled. "I just finished eating an hour ago." She pouted and glanced at clock. It read 11am.

She had just finished eating pizza and toast and now she was craving mashed potatoes and ice-cream and it wasn't even lunch time yet.

A knock came on the door.

"Who is it?" Jane asked as she rubbed her stomach.

"It's Martha."

Jane smiled thanking God that her secretary came at the right time. "Come in."

"Ma'am, a man by the name of Ben Pratt is here to see you."

Jane frowned at the information wondering why Ben was there to see her and how he knew her office.

"Let him in and... please get me some mashed potatoes and ice-cream."

She looks surprised by Jane's request, "But ma'am I got you pizza and French toast a few hours ago."

"Yes now I want something else."

She sighed and left.

Jane knew that it hadn't gone unnoticed to her colleagues that her eating habits had changed and in the process she had gained weight. She could sometimes hear the snide remarks she got as she walked by with some of them calling her a pig. However, she wasn't going to ignore her cravings and starve herself just because of other people's opinion.

Ben entered into her office smiling.

"Finally! I get to see you again," he said as he embraced her. She wondered when they had gotten so close for him to hug her.

"I'm surprised you know where I work"

"Well I have my ways."

"Please have a sit."

He obliged and sat down in front of her.

"What brings you here?" Jane asked curiously.

"You." His answer shocks her and she give him a questioning look.

He bursts out in laughte.r "I'm just joking but it's not far from the truth."

He sat up and straightened in his seat.

"I was looking forward to seeing you on that business trip with Ethan but he was alone and you were nowhere in sight. It was then I knew there was trouble in paradise."

Her heart raced as she pondered on what to say to counter his words. Nobody was supposed to know that they were no longer together.

"He was a mess on that trip. He spent time drinking and smoking until he lost the deal. I thought he would hook up with the ladies throwing themselves at him but I was surprised when he didn't. He really has it bad for you."

"Why are you here?" she asked wondering why he was talking about Ethan when everyone knew that they were frenemies.

"Good question." He folded his arms and leaned back on the chair

"Only a few set of people know that you guys are separated. If I must tell you I was glad because I have a crush on you. But seeing him so depressed and broken, I just had to see you."

He paused for a moment as if thinking over his next words.

"I've been in your guys shoes before. I let her go because I was a coward and too afraid to face my feelings but here I am still hurting while she has a family now."

"Tell it to Ethan." She didn't want to hear about this.

"I tried but he won't listen to me."

"Well, I'm the wrong person to talk to," she snapped.

"He pushed me away. I can't go back to someone who doesn't love me or respect me."

She could feel a headache coming. She rubbed her forehead with her hands while Ben looked on worried.

"Are you all right?" he asked in concern.

"Yeah I'm fine. It's just a headache."

He studied your face for a moment and shook his head. "You're not fine. I can see the dark circles under your eyes. You haven't been sleeping, Janelle."

"Why are you acting, as if you know me?" she was getting pissed off now.

He raised his hands up in defense. "I'm just trying to help."

She was about to tell him that he was not helping when her dad barged in, banging the door behind him.

"Dad?" she stood up in shock as she watched her fuming dad.

"Don't you dare dad me. What is this?" he asked as he showed her his phone screen.

She gave him a skeptical look before glancing at the phone and reading the content out loud

"Well known billionaire, Ethan Smith's marriage has hit the rocks in just three months. Click here for more details."

"Is this why you've been spending late nights at the office? Is Ethan already tired of you?" he asked as he withdrew his phone from her sight.

She kept quiet unable to say anything in her defense.

"I think you should just calm down and discuss this issue like normal adults," Ben suggested sensing the tension in the room.

"And who are you?"

"I'm ..." Ben was cut off by Jane's father.

"I don't give a damn about who you are but if you have any manners you will know that you shouldn't meddle in family matters."

"I can't just sit here and watch you talk to her like that!"

She couldn't stand the shouting and the arguments anymore. Her migraine was getting worse and she was starting to feel dizzy.

"Please stop," she managed to say as she blinked trying to keep herself awake.

"Are you all right?" Ben was now standing by her side holding onto her hands.

She wanted to say that she was fine, that there was nothing to worry about but the next thing she saw was black.

Ben quickly caught her before she hit the floor, carrying her immediately in a bridal style.

"Jane!" Mr. Payne yelled her name as he rushed to her side.

"Call an ambulance!" Ben yelled at Mr. Payne who looked around confused for a moment before he dashed out.

Chapter 8

"You've got to stop doing this?" Ryan said as he stared at his friend, Ethan who had just woken up after spending the night drinking. He was lying on the bed staring at the ceiling as if there was something written on it that caught his attention.

"Stop what?" Ethan asked still not taking his eyes away from the ceiling.

"This pity party. You guys had a stupid fight which can still be resolved if you act like a man and just tell her that you love her," Ryan almost yelled. He was frustrated with his friend's antics.

Ethan had become a shadow of himself since he pushed Jane away. He had abandoned his company, his friends and drowned himself in alcohol and weed just to forget her and Ryan was tired of it. He was tired of babysitting Ethan.

"You didn't want to hurt her but you ended up hurting her. Are you happy now? That woman has loved you even before she knew what love was. She has always been by your side, through your pains and tribulations. She was always there and you just had to be a coward and chase her away because you are too afraid to accept that you have fallen for her," he yelled this time not holding anything back.

This time Ethan looked at him and sat up. "Why are you yelling at me?"

Ryan stood up from where he sat at the left side of the bed and bent down to look at Ethan. "Because I'm trying to knock some sense into you!"

"Your greatest fear has come true because you have turned into your mother!"

Ethan winced hating that he was right. Everyone was right. He was an asshole who hated his mother but he was just the same.

"I just hope it won't take too long for you to come to your senses because I won't be there to console you when she ends up with a better man!"

"Is there something you are not telling me?" Ethan asked suddenly finding interest in Ryan's outburst. He couldn't picture Jane with another man. He just couldn't.

Ryan was about to say something when his phone rang breaking the silence. He dipped his hands into his pocket and brought out his phone.

"It's Ben," Ryan said as he stared at the caller's Id.

Ethan frowned wondering why Ben would contact Ryan.

Ryan picked the call while Ethan watched as Ryan's expression changed from skeptical to worried.

"What? How is she? Yeah I'm my way." Ryan cut the call and stared at his phone for a moment.

"What happened?" Ethan asked worried. He hated being kept in the dark and something told him the news was meant for him.

Ryan looked up to meet his gaze and shook his head. "Jane fainted and was rushed to the hospital."

"what?" Ethan jumped out of bed "We have to go. Where are my car keys?" he asked as he dug into his pockets for his car keys.

"I'll drive. I can't let you drive in your state." Ryan pointed at him while Ethan looked down at himself. He knew he looked a mess but he didn't give a damn.

He rushed downstairs after Ryan who quickly grabbed his car keys from the dining table.

They dashed out of the house and entered the car. Ryan ignited the car engine and drove out of the mansion headed for the hospital.

"Will you drive faster," Ethan suggested wanting to get there as soon as possible.

"I'm trying my best, okay. Will you please stop panicking. It's not helping," Ryan said his eyes focused on the road as he drove.

"You could've just allowed me to drive."

Ryan scoffed. "Excuse me for not wanting to die before my time."

"See, we're here," Ryan declared as he pulled up to the hospital and parked his car in the parking lot.

Ethan wasted no time in getting out of the car and rushing inside the hospital. He saw a nurse behind the counter and rushed to her panting.

"Please do you know which ward Janelle Smith is admitted to? I'm her husband," he asked desperation evident in his voice.

"Hey Ethan, it's not cool that you left me out there," Ryan said as he walked in

"Can you please be fast about it?" he told the nurse who was still scanning through the register.

"Ethan?" he heard his name being called and turned to the direction of the voice only to spot Ben.

"Where is she?" Ethan asked anger laced in his voice.

"Hey, calm down."

"Calm down? What did you do to her?" He was trying to keep his cool even though it was taking every will power in him not to punch Ben.

"I didn't do anything. She fainted in her office and I brought her here."

He sighed. "Look I'll take you there. Just follow me," he said while they followed him into the hospital.

Mr. Payne was seated on the visitor's seat his head on his hands when he heard footsteps approaching. He looked up in time to see the three men walking toward him with Ethan leading the way.

"Is she okay?" Ethan asked Mr. Payne in concern.

Mr. Payne sighed and shook his head. "I don't know. We just rushed her here and the doctor hasn't said anything yet."

Just then the door to the room where Jane was confined opened and the doctor walked out smiling.

"How is she?" Ethan asked.

The doctor smiled at him. "You don't have to worry about her, she's perfectly fine."

The doctor paused for a minute and looked between the four men. "Which one of you is her husband?" he asked.

Ethan stepped forward. "I am."

The doctor extended his hands out for a handshake while Ethan looked on confused. "Congratulations, Your wife is pregnant."

His eyes widened as he took several steps back suddenly losing his brain cells.

"She's pregnant?" Mr. Payne asked rhetorically still shocked by the revelation.

"Yes she is."

"But why did she faint?" Ryan asked.

"She fainted due to stress and lack of vitamins but there's nothing to worry about. She just has to start her prenatal care."

"Guy, you are a sharp shooter," Ryan chuckled while nudging Ethan.

"Can I see her now?" Ethan asked after finding his voice. He couldn't believe he was going to be a father. It all sounded like a dream. All he wanted to do now was to bombard Jane with kisses.

"Yes you can," the doctor said. "Only one person for now."

Ethan followed the doctor inside the room.

Jane blinked several times to confirm that she was indeed seeing Ethan. He was there right in front of her, staring at her like she was some trophy that he had won.

"What is he doing here?" she asked the doctor as she pointed at Ethan.

"He said he's your husband and I just told him that you are pregnant."

She couldn't believe her ears. "I'm pregnant? This must be a joke. How is that even possible I've been seeing my period?" she asked the doctor.

"You just experienced decidual bleeding, ma'am. We've carried out the necessary tests and determined that you and your baby are in perfect health."

Jane stared at the doctor, then at Ethan who was already staring at her.

"How can I be pregnant?" she asked herself. She hadn't planned on this. It wasn't part of their plan. She scoffed. Having sex was not part of their plans either but they had broken all the rules in the contract.

"Jane," Ethan called as he finally gathered the courage to move closer to her.

"Don't you dare come near me," she warned. She didn't want to see him. This was too much for her to digest.

"I'm sorry. I'm really, really sorry," he pleaded as his eyes tearing up.

"No! Stay away from me. Get out!" she yelled startling him.

"Please just go." she pleaded on the brink of tears. This wasn't how she wanted her year to be. She wasn't ready to be a mother especially for a man who didn't love her.

He nodded getting the message and walked out of the room.

"Ethan, we need to talk," Mr. Payne said.

"About what?"

"You and my daughter."

Ethan crossed his arms ready to hear what Jane's father had to say.

Mr. Payne cleared his throat as he studied the young man in front of him for a second before sighing. "Before your father made his will, he called me aside and voiced his concern on how you were wasting your life away being a workaholic and a womanizer without having a woman by your side."

Ethan frowned and bit his lips. He could definitely imagine his father saying that.

"He felt guilty for being the one who made you distrustful of women. He didn't want to leave this world knowing that you would be alone so he asked me to make that will."

"Do you know why he chose Jane?" Mr. Payne asked while Ethan shook his head. He didn't know but he was dying to know.

"He couldn't find a better woman for you than Jane. She was the only woman you allowed to be close to you and he wanted that to stay forever. He didn't want you to lose her forever so he made that will."

He placed a hand on Ethan's shoulder, squeezing it reassuringly. "Don't make your dad regret making that decision."

"Why are you acting like her dad all of a sudden?" Ethan asked as he couldn't believe that Mr. Payne was actually advising him on treating Jane better; when he had spent his whole life maltreating his daughter and blaming her for her mother's death.

Mr. Payne sighed as he withdrew his hand from Ethan's shoulder. "It's never too late to repent son."

"It's never too late," Mr. Payne said as he walked away.

Epilogue

"Dad!" A five year old boy yelled as he ran across the field chasing his puppy. He slipped on the wet grass and let out a loud cry when his father rushed to him and scooped him up, swaying him from side to side.

"Don't cry, baby," he whispered while swaying his son.

"I'm not a baby," the boy said as he wiped his tears.

The man chuckled and said, "Big boys don't cry."

"I'm not crying. Something just entered my eye," the boy said while his father laughed putting his son down. The boy was so stubborn like him and it amazed him every time how the boy was too much like him. He had his blond hair and his blue eyes but he also had his mother's beauty and smile.

Speaking of his mother, a heavily pregnant woman dressed in an oversized white top and blue jeans matched with trainers walked into the field fuming.

"Ethan, how many times have I told you not to allow him to play here?" Jane asked fuming.

Ethan sighed and brushed his hair back "I'm sorry."

She frowned and crossed her arms. "That's what you said the last time."

"Jane, relax, he's just a little boy. Let him have fun."

She rolled her eyes. "He can have the fun he wants inside and not on the wet grass. I don't want him to get hurt."

"Mom I'm okay, " the boy said holding onto her leg. "You nag too much."

Her mouth opened wide in surprise as she stared between father and son. Ethan couldn't help but laugh at his son's comment.

She raised her hands up in defeat. "I don't even know why I bother with you guys. Like father like son." She made to leave but he hugged her from behind preventing her from leaving.

"Babe, I'm sorry." He apologized and pecked her cheeks. He knew it was her pregnancy hormones affecting her mood.

She melted into his embrace reveling in his touch.

"I don't know why I put up with you." she smiled.

"Because you love me."

They both chuckled remembering an incident from five years ago.

"Why are you here?" Jane asked Ethan who had just walked into her apartment like he owned the place while holding onto a bouquet of lilies, her favorite flower.

"To see you," he said it like it was the most obvious thing in the world.

She had been avoiding him for a week since they both found out that she was pregnant. He simply took advantage of the opportunity that her door was open and walked in.

"Well you've seen me, now go."

"Jane," he called.

"Are you here to see the result of our one night stand or to blame me for planning this and trapping you with a baby?"

He stared at her incredulously.

"If this is about the baby, I'm keeping it. You don't have to take responsibility as the father. I'm okay by myself."

He groaned. "Why are you putting words in my mouth?"

"Then what else are you here for?"

He placed the bouquet on the table and said, "To apologize for being a jerk and pushing you away."

She rolled her eyes and folded her arms

"I didn't mean what I said that night. I thought I was doing the right thing by pushing you away but I ended up hurting us both."

"Is that all?"

"No Jane listen to me. I love you. I always have and it's such a pity that it took a kiss for me to realize it. That night wasn't a mistake. It meant much more to me, so much more that it scared me and I just chose the easier way out by pushing you away because I was too afraid to face my feelings."

He couldn't read her facial expression. He wasn't even sure if she was listening but he wasn't going to stop now.

"I love you, Jane. I really do but I'll understand if you don't feel the same anymore but please let me in my child's life," he pleaded.

She just stood there staring at him blankly.

"I'm sorry. I'll just go," He said as he turned to leave.

"Ethan," she called and he stopped in his tracks and turned to face her.

"I love you too." She threw herself at him while he embraced her as if he was afraid that she would slip away. They stayed like that for a few minutes until she pulled out of the hug.

"Took you two months to apologize."

"Nah, it took me two months, three weeks and two days."

She opened her mouth in surprise. "You've been counting it."

"Yeah, I couldn't help it. It's been hell without you."

"Remind me why I put up with you." she asked as she leaned her head against his.

"Because you love me," he chuckled earning a playful punch in return.

***

"Don't you think we should make another baby?" he whispered in her ear causing her to shiver.

She rolled her eyes and chuckled. "I'm already pregnant at least let me push this one out first."

"it's not too late," he said as he nuzzled her neck, taking in her fragrance.

"Mom, Dad let's go inside. I'm feeling cold," Edward said as he pouted interrupting his parent's moment.

Ethan reluctantly released Jane with a groan while the later stifled a laugh.

Edward ran inside with his mother trailing after him while Ethan stayed behind in order to catch the puppy.

He smiled at the retreating back of his son. He had named his son Edward after his father. The man who had made sure he didn't end up alone. He looked up at the sky and muttered a thank you to his dad.

His father had given him the will to love and he would never trade this all for anything.

THE END

The Alien Project

Description

Some sort of government project was initiated after a series of extremely secret findings on Venus. Vagrants, criminals, drug-addicts... all of them had been some form of undesirable or another, taken because they wouldn't be missed. Clara found herself on this same planet and a prisoner for experiment. The strangest stuff came from the oldest residents.

As her time in the facility lengthened, Clara began to both fear and wish to be the next one taken. It seemed that the longer you were in before you got selected, the worse the experience was. Not until she was taken and had to deal with an alien, with pain and pleasure.

Chapter 1

"TZZSSSSSSHhhhhHhhtt-rotocol 9, initiating at 1500 hours. Subject C-V-19, batch 2."

Sterile white light momentarily blinded Clara, making her blink beadily. She had been at the facility for almost 7 months now, long enough to have become familiar with its procedures from the other men, women, and even children kept trapped here. It was all so complicated, so muddled, that she hardly knew what to believe. After all the things she had seen, there was little that seemed beyond the realm of reality.

What she DID know was that this was all some sort of government project, initiated after a series of extremely secret findings on Venus. Clara had heard all kinds of strange tales from the other people here. Vagrants, criminals, drug-addicts... all of them had been some form of undesirable or another, taken because they wouldn't be missed.

Clara spent a lot of time doing nothing. The rest of the prisoners would talk, play word games, and otherwise try to fill empty time. Any sort of physical contact, even just a hand on the shoulder, was prohibited.

The strangest stuff came from the oldest residents. Each person had a different story of what happened in that place, each more bizarre and awful than the last. Whatever the scientists here were trying to accomplish, it seemed to have no rhyme or reason.

As her time in the facility lengthened, Clara began to both fear and wish to be the next one taken. It seemed that the longer you were in before you got selected, the worse the experience was.

Finally, one day, it was her turn. Clara was taken to some kind of prep room, bathed, and ordered into a sort of white bodysuit. The rest of the time, the prisoner wore thin plasticky tunics and pants reminiscent of scrubs, so in truth it *was actually kind of nice to feel actual cloth against her skin. Then she was taken into another room, where she was strapped to an X-shaped metal table and injected full of a rainbow's worth of serums and fluids. She had no idea what any of them were, and any questions were met with stony silence. A metallic taste grew in her mouth, and Clara began to sweat.*

Whatever they had given her was decidedly unpleasant. Her eyes stung, but she seemed incapable of producing tears. It was like every drop of fluid in her body was pouring out through her pores. Clara began to swear, then yell, but the scientists only muttered to each other and fitted her with an array of sensors.

Thoroughly secured, the workers left the room. When the lights flickered off, Clara was left to scream in the dark. Beyond the gap there was nothing but more darkness as far as Clara could tell with her limited view. On and on she went down this narrow metal shaft, to the point that she started feeling rather claustrophobic.

Finally, the gurney came to a halt. A pause, and then brilliant white lights dazzled her. Bored voices hissed over the intercom, rattling off strings of letters and numbers that meant nothing to Clara's untrained ears. More suited and masked scientists, some with imposing-looking guns, were scattered around the room. And there, in the center, the infamous obsidian egg. It looked almost like a massive, rough-hewn gem, faceted and uneven, but overall, a relatively even shape.

Near the top was a crown of black spikes, like crystals. It must have been at least twenty-five feet across and easily half again that in height. Other than the beeps and hums of the machinery surrounding it, the object itself appeared inert. Clara imagined she could see some kind of glinting purple light at its heart, but that was more likely than not the product of whatever cocktail she had been shot up with.

After a few moments of busy activity, all the agents cleared out of the room. The intercom hissed to life again.

The bright lights vanished. Now there was only the sound of machines... and...? A soft clicking, insectoid and vaguely wet somehow, under the beep and hum of computers. Clara whipped her head to the side, trying to track it.

"H-hey!"

The clicking faded, and then resumed, closer, more insistent. It was accompanied by the sound of a scurrying tak-tak-tak-tak-taktaktaktak, as of someone (or something) with claws hurrying across a hard surface.

"HEY! There's something in here! Can you bastards hear me?! THERE'S SOMETHING IN HERE!"

"There is nothing in the room with you."

Clara spasmed, a swooping tingle not unlike what one experienced during vertigo running down her spine. She had heard something speak in her mind. The voice was distant, as though it were echoing up from the bottom of a well, yet simultaneously terribly intimate. Clara had the sense that if she just whipped her head around fast enough, she might catch the speaker whispering in her ear.

"They are trying to frighten you your mind and body are full of chemicals and they are deceiving your senses and muddying your thoughts."

"Hello!? Who - who's there? Who are you?!"

There was no answer, and Clara's breathing seemed loud to her own ears. It was hard to tell if the voice was a hallucination of her own fevered mind, or another trick by the inhumane researchers. The idea that it was real was too frightening to even contemplate.

"Do not fear me," a voice responded.

Clara's eyes roved unseeing, imagining writhing demons in the dark. Monsters. But the voice was so cool and soothing, like a balm to her battered mind. It felt strange, but Clara was desperate for a lifeline. Anything to bring peace to her thoughts. The speaker, it seemed, could sense her frantic groping for a semblance of calm.

Who are you?

"I am Uldra, from another world."

"You're whatever they found on Venus. The egg thing. You're an alien," Clara said.

"Yes."

What do they want with you? With me? What is going on? I'm so confused, I can't think straight. You can get us out?

"I need your help but willingly you must help but you are so afraid. Open to me."

Clara gasped, her mind overwhelmed with sights and sounds. Between the confusion brought on by the drugs administered to her and the entirely alien experience of having someone speak to her telepathically, it was all a bit much. Clara felt faint. Uldra... had somehow transferred its memories to her.

It was like a dream where you just know something, without any explanation. Clara could see images and feel things associated with them; she could know instantly the exact way Uldra had felt at that moment in time. She could feel her own sense of identity blurring as the flood of information kept coming.

Humans had found life on Venus, something they had not expected. Uldra and its kind were few in number, immensely long-lived and physically hardy, designed to survive the brutal environment of their home planet. Things had gone predictably awry, and Uldra's kinfolk had driven off the humans through violence. Uldra had been wounded, and retreated into this husk form to recover, but humans had returned and essentially kidnapped it.

Uldra had almost died upon entering Earth's atmosphere, something the government officials tasked with transporting it had clearly counted on. It was only the stasis sleep it was in that protected it, providing speeded healing and adaptation. Its survival, however, was far from guaranteed, as it had been locked away in this facility ever since. Subjected to tests day in, day out, Uldra had stubbornly remained uncommunicative and dormant ever since, waiting for a chance to escape. Clara, it seemed, was that chance.

However, the particulars of what this escape would entail were rather...frightening, to say the least. Uldra was very insistent that only willing participation would create the necessary circumstances, but... essentially, they needed to mate. Uldra could not survive for long in Earth's atmosphere outside of stasis without modifying its genome, which it could only do through sex.

Uldra admitted that it was not confident this would even work with a human, as its own species was so entirely unlike Clara's, but it was willing to try. If Clara, too, proved willing, Uldra would risk it all for the escape attempt.

Uldra said that the researchers had no idea Uldra's kind were sapient, and that Clara could use this to her advantage to ease the proceedings.

If she told them what Uldra wanted, but not why, they would no doubt eagerly encourage the coupling out of scientific interest, morbid curiosity, and just plain relief at finally having something happen.

When Clara idly thought *Why me?* Uldra seemed to feel... something like embarrassment? According to it, her particular brain was built just so to be receptive to Uldra's *thoughts without negative consequences. And... Uldra had liked the scent of her.*

The idea of some kind of ridiculous alien monster being shy made Clara burst into wild, sudden laughter. She would have restrained herself, but the scientists thought she was bugging out on drugs anyway, so what the hell?

What would this... mating... entail? Will it hurt?

No, Uldra informed her, in fact in theory it would be pleasant for her. Uldra would be learning to match human biochemistry throughout, and releasing a mix of pheromones and chemicals designed to heighten arousal. It would be as gentle as possible, it promised, considering their size difference.

Size difference? What do you look like?

Chapter 2

Again, that vague shyness, a reluctance to frighten her. Uldra, as it turned out, looked much like a massive spider. Clara couldn't suppress a shudder, and felt a wave of apologetic sympathy. She, in turn, felt surprisingly guilty. This inter-planetary spider horror was being nicer to her than most humans in her life ever had been.

She felt bad for her instinctive revulsion. She tried to focus on the image presented to her. With a little consideration, Uldra was not so bad. It didn't have hairs, like earth spiders. Instead, it was all smooth and shiny black, glassy like the egg that it currently occupied. It had a smaller, more angular head, more like a wasp.

In addition to its primary six legs, it had six more smaller ones clasped close under its body. The whole of it scintillated blackly, gleaming with deep purples, blues, and greens. Iridescent, like spilled gasoline on asphalt. Uldra's many multifaceted eyes were black and seemed to glow from within.

Okay, okay. That's... not so bad.

"I can feel the deep genetic fear inside you but I appreciate your kindness," the voice continued.

Was the space-spider being vaguely sardonic? Wonders never ceased. Clara thought for a little while, weighing her options. Sometimes, people she had seen here would disappear. She very much doubted they were being sent home with an apology card.

The only reason you used the fringe of society for your sick experiments was if you wanted to be able to make people go away without consequence. Her future looked grim; there was no way she could escape on her own, and the chances of being freed looked mighty slim. Uldra might be her only chance of getting out alive, and as far as psychic cosmic aberrations went, it seemed pleasant enough.

"H - hey? Science guys? I think your egg is talking to me."

The intercom hissed on instantly. Clara felt a vague, contemptuous anger. Of course pleading and screaming in terror had no response, but news about their precious pet experiment? Ugh. She laughed, the sound forced and humorless, but that worked for the situation. It took little effort to sound like she was scared and trying to hide it.

"I think it wants to fuck," she added

There were a few tense heartbeats of silence.

"How is it speaking, C-V-19? Is it using human speech?"

"No... I don't think it's capable of that. It's not really talking, more like... beaming horny feelings at me? I don't know. How would a dog express amorous intent toward a leg?"

"Stand by. Initiating protocol 17."

The lights came on, not the bright floodlights of before but a dim glow. Clara was grateful, as it was easy on her eyes. The intercom was still on, but it sounded like the researchers had moved away from it. Even so, the snippets of their conversation drifted through the mic.

"Let the thing fuck her? I have to admit, I'm kind of curi..."

"Anything at this point. At least it's some kind of response..."

"Starting to think it was dead after all. Alright, yes, let's. Do we have..."

"Should make proceedings go more smoothly. Might bring some home to the missus if you..."

They appeared to have come to an agreement. After a moment, there was a tinny beep, and a delicate robotic arm *unfolded from under the table. It extended a thin needle and jabbed Clara in the bicep, making her wince. Twice, something cold and prickly flooded into her veins, followed by a steady drip of cool fluid that made Clara shiver.*

"Following indications of an intent to mate, subject C-V-19 was dosed with a clearing mix to remove any remaining traces of L2, and then dosed with set C6 instead. Rehydration initiated through saline."

What "set C6" did, Clara supposed she would have to wait to find out. She supposed what was flooding into her arm now was saline, to alleviate the dehydration she was supposedly experiencing. She had been sweating a lot, hadn't she? She drily thought to herself that it was no wonder Uldra had smelled her even in the depths of a fucking magic alien coma.

"You smell nice anyway if it's any comfort," the alien said.

Comforting, indeed. As Clara lay there, she began to be aware of a strange tingling in her fingers and toes. The cotton body suit felt strangely rough all of a sudden, as though her skin had doubled in sensitivity. Her thoughts felt a bit wooly, languid and slow. Most bizarrely, Clara could feel the uncomfortably insistent pressure of arousal growing between her legs. Of course. "C6" must be a batch of aphrodisiacs. The saline drip was withdrawn, but Clara barely noticed. In the last 20 minutes, she had found herself increasingly horny.

She could feel her pussy getting wet, and the bodysuit seemed to rasp like sandpaper against her hard and suddenly incredibly sensitive nipples. Clara was of a small frame, compact and wiry. Lots of running would do that to you. Her legs were pleasantly firm with muscle, and she had a flat stomach and pert, smallish breasts capped with quarter-sized little pink nipples like pencil erasers.

She kept her black hair cut jaggedly short out of convenience, though in her time here it had grown out enough to brush her shoulders. Clara had a fast as hard and angular as her body, though when she smiled it would soften to reveal a radiant, energetic sort of beauty. Despite being only 26, her blue eyes were nestled amongst crow's feet born of both hard living and a surprising amount of laughter for such. Freckles dusted the bridge of her pointed, upturned nose.

Her attention was drawn sharply to the great egg when a resounding crack rang out like a gunshot.

"It's working! The creature is finally stirring! Are the cameras recording? Make sure all of them are recording!" The scientist sounded breathless with excitement; his eagerness almost unseemly. For her own part, trepidation and vague fear warred with hope and arousal in Clara's mind.

The massive structure before her had cracked in three places, jagged lines running from the crest to the floor. They burst open explosively, taking out a good portion of the equipment near it. Shards of glassy eggshell smashed to the floor. A long, delicate leg unfolded from the wreckage.

Uldra was even bigger than Clara imagined, unfolding to stand even taller than the egg. The chamber was dwarfed by its size, easily 35 feet in height. Its sharp legs seemed too thin to support its mass, and they rang out like bells when they struck the steel floor. Even as Clara began to question how this arrangement could possibly work, the concoction inside her was insisting that it would, somehow. A horny mammal knew no obstacles to sex.

Slowly, almost majestically, Uldra lowered itself over Clara. One sharp, massive leg reached out and seemed to just tap the steel cuffs holding her to the table. With a screech of rending metal, they fell away. Clara suddenly became very aware of just how much more fragile her soft human body was than a sheet of tempered steel.

Uldra, however, seemed aware of that too. The alien reached toward her with the smaller graspers on its underside, gathering Clara close to its body. To her surprise, Uldra wasn't cold, but in fact pleasantly warm. There was a strange shifting, and some sort of plate seemed to slide away. Clara found herself facing the floor, her back to something soft and almost velvety.

It appeared that for mating, Uldra could retract its armored shell to expose... something. Clara figured that made sense. Humans changed physically for mating, too.

With surgeon-like precision, the graspers sliced away and discarded the cotton bodysuit. Clara felt terribly exposed, but her state of arousal was such that she didn't much care. The air on her bare skin felt wonderful, and so did Uldra's soft and plush underbelly.

Then things started to get really interesting.

From somewhere behind her, long black tentacles snaked around her body. They seemed to take over for the hard and unyielding graspers in supporting her, coiling around her arms, legs, and waist. They were thick and vaguely slimy, though the texture felt pleasant against her skin. As she watched, a multitude of thinner tendrils began to stroke her flesh, sliding along her body.

As Uldra was no doubt still tuned in to her mind, Clara found she only had to think 'oh, that's nice', for the tentacles to arrange themselves exactly to her liking. Having a psychic lover, even a monstrous, alien one, clearly had its upsides.

The thinner tendrils, capped with some kind of suckers, affixed themselves to Clara's nipples. She moaned, her nerves on fire, and felt the tentacles pulling and twisting the sensitive nubs. The thicker ones tightened around her breasts, squeezing them forward and making her already stiff nipples hard. The swollen red tips were momentarily released, eliciting a gasp of disappointment from Clara, before being attacked again.

Pulled, twisted, and pinched, Uldra kept up a varying and mismatched rhythm that somehow gave Clara exactly what she wanted while also leaving her achingly unsatisfied. One nipple would experience rough, erotic abuse, pulled taut until Clara cried out with a delighted mixture of pain and pleasure, while the other would only be lightly flicked and teased.

Then, switch. Clara's pussy was already maddeningly wet, slick pussy juices running down her slit to bead on her engorged, pink clit and drip slowly to the floor far below. Distantly, she could head the intercom keeping up a running commentary. The observers sounded breathless with more than just academic excitement.

"Look at how it's teasing her. It's clearly reading her body somehow; how else would it know to stimulate her nipples so roughly? It's squeezing her tits to force blood into them and make them more sensitive. Ung- Her pussy is fucking soaking wet, look. Zoom in on camera 7. Look at that. I've never seen a cunt more desperate to get fucked."

The idea that her twitching pussy was being closely inspected while Clara hung there helpless, legs spread, only served to excite her more. Tendrils were snaking their way down between her legs now, and she let out a needful moan.

"A — ah, yes... ahh, tease my pussy... God, I want it so bad, I'm so wet! Fuck!"

Clara desperately wanted to be filled and fucked, yet the buildup was exciting her in ways she had never imagined. Delicately probing tentacles found her clit, and a sucker latched on to the sensitive nub, swollen with arousal. Clara threw her head back in ecstasy, crying out. This tendril pulsed and suckled rhythmically, before slowly beginning to pull and squeeze her clit.

The bundle of nerves was agonizingly sensitive, and Clara shuddered and spasmed in Uldra's grasp. Between the concoction given to her by the scientists, and whatever pheromones and chemicals Uldra was secreting, she was being driven to distraction. Clara had never felt so mindlessly horny, so desperate for all kinds of depraved things that normally would never have crossed her mind. Well, the thoughts were there now, and Uldra was perfectly equipped to read and fulfill them.

"N-no it's... it's too sensitive... ahh, it feels so...so good, it hurts, nngh... aahnnnnn - not my clit, nno..."

Despite her words, the teasing and torture of the overly-sensitive organ was unbelievably arousing. Hanging there helpless, the pleasure reaching an intensity that hurt, Clara found her cunt aching to be filled like never before. She continued to protest weakly, her "god no"s and "please not there"s punctuated by groans of ecstasy. The more Uldra played with her tits and pussy, the more Clara struggled, but also the more she enjoyed the inability to get away from the torturous attentions of the tireless tentacles.

She could freely use all her strength without a hint of being able to free herself. That in itself was even relaxing, in a way, as Clara could completely lose herself without the worries about hurting Uldra the way she would with a human lover.

The tendril was joined by a second, and the first sucker pulled her clit out painfully far while the second curled around it, stroking and squeezing. Clara bucked and moaned, but Uldra's grasp was resolute. No matter how her aching, abused clit and tits were squeezed, sucked, and twisted, Clara could not escape the tentacles ministrations.

"Auhh, my clit... oh fuck... ahh - it's so sensitive, God, it hurts so good... nnno... don't suck it any more... my swollen little clit can't take it..."

"Are we getting everything? Listen to her, she's moaning like crazy. Listen to her talk about her clit getting teased, she loves it. Her cunt is the wettest I've ever seen!"

Clara moaned loudly, the act of talking about her own body being played with and knowing it was being watched terribly arousing. She could feel her clit and nipples ache with each beat of her heart, blood flooding into them. Her nipples were puffy and red from their harsh treatment, and her swollen clit protruded from her pussy lips, inviting further torment. When the tentacles stopped, Clara was forced to beg for the very thing she had just pleaded to end.

"Uhhnn, my clit... need to be played with... please, it's aching! Ung, god, please suck and tease my clit... it's so swollen and sensitive... unng, my pussy needs to be punished and filled... please... I want you to torture my clit... play with it... unnahh..."

The tentacle returned, pinching her clit hard, flicking and suckling on it.

"Oh god, yes! Unng, ahh, ah, it hurts, oh it's so sensitive, unhh it feels so good! Punish my aching little clit!"

"Listen to her beg for it, this wet little slut is enjoying every second of getting tormented by this monster. Fuck, it's so hot. I'm gonna save these tapes for later... watch her get violated from every angle..."

Then Clara felt something stroking the entrance to her hot, wet pussy. A tentacle, thicker than the others, slowly pushed its way inside her tight entrance. Her cunt twitched and clamped down on the thick tentacle, loving the sensation. Clara cried out at once, the orgasm wracking her body making her see white. Thick, sticky pussy juice dripped past the appendage penetrating her. She went momentarily limp, but even throughout this the tendrils on her nipples and clit did not stop for a moment.

"She just came, the sensors are going wild. She came from that thing just entering her cunt, not even fucking her. I can't believe this wet little slut, she must have been a hair away from cumming before that tentacle slid inside her pussy. Look, it's barely even started..."

It was true. The tentacle throbbed, growing slightly thicker and thinner in turn, rhythmically pulsating as it worked its way deeper inside her. Clara groaned, her pussy feeling delightfully full.

"Ahh, yes, nice and deep... nnnhhh, yes, please... fill up my pussy, ohh, it's so good... more..."

To her happy surprise, the first tentacle was joined by a second. Deeper and deeper they writhed, until Clara could feel them nudging her cervix. One would slide in while the other slide out, the unusual pattern making her beg for more. No human cock could possibly match this pleasure. A third tentacle stroked the outside of her pussy before slowly beginning to force its way inside.

Clara cried out, her tight little entrance feeling stretched to its limits. Still, the tentacle went in further and further. Clara loved the sensation, and when she felt a particularly rough twist on her nipples, the combined sensation of her painfully full, sopping went cunt and her abused tits made her scream in orgasm once more.

"She came again, that fucking cockslut. Holy shit, look at how it's stretching her pussy. And she's taking all of it, and loving it. This has to be more than just our chemicals... I've never seen a cunt get stuffed like that. And look, oh fuck..."

A fourth tentacle was pressing insistently at her entrance, while a fifth... had snaked between her legs and was probing her ass.

"N-no! Unng, not... no... I can't... I'm so full, my pussy... it's being, aahhn, stretched so much... nnghuaah, no! Noo... so full... not in there, not my ass... uah, my little cunt... you're filling my tight little fuckhole, I can't take anymore!"

The fourth tentacle squirmed inside her, and Clara could feel it throbbing and pulsing. Her pussy twitched and clenched around it, achingly full. Sticky pussy juices slicked her thighs, her arousal reaching a new high.

The fifth, slimy tendril pushed, and then slowly slid inside her virgin ass. Clara cried out in protest, but her writhing was to no avail. Deeper and deeper the intruding appendage forced its way in, pulsating and thickening as it went. Unbelievably, a second tentacle slowly began to join the first, twining around it. Clara had never had her ass fucked in any way, let alone violated like this. The flexible tentacles could force their way deeper into her than any stiff cock or toy ever could.

"Not... so full... unggh, my pussy and ass getting fucked... nnhh, I'm being stretched so much, I can't take it... I can't... no... no more..."

Her weak protests were cut off when a tentacle snaked inside her mouth. To Clara's surprise, it tasted rather pleasant, vaguely like vanilla. The thick tendril reduced her cries to muffled incoherence, so that when a third tentacle began to work its way into her ass, she could only moan and squirm. She could only imagine what her pussy and ass must look like, filled with squirming, thrusting tentacles.

Four in her pussy and three in her ass, thick and deep inside, fucking her like never before. Clara had never been so aroused, so desperately needing release.

The third tendril in her ass squirmed deeper and deeper, joining the other two. Clara guessed that she must have had at least 9 or 10 inches in her pussy, painfully deep and thick, and at least a good 15 or even 16 in her ass, curving and thrusting to get even deeper.

"I can't believe it, look at how she's taking all those things in her pussy and ass. Ngh, god, it's fucking every hole... how much more can this little slut take? Her cunt must be practically tearing, and it hasn't let up on her tits or clit this whole time... Look, it's spreading her legs wider... do you think...? Yeah, look! It's gonna use another one... lets see where it puts it, pussy or ass? Do you think her pussy can take any more? O-oh... looks like it'll have too... mm, look at that, it's gotta go slow. Must be a struggle getting anything more inside that full, sopping wet cunt, stretched as it is..."

Clara could only listen and moan helplessly as a fifth tendril, thick and demanding, slowly pushed its way inside her entrance. Her pussy was stretched painfully wide, creamy juice dripping freely. As the fifth tentacle agonizingly thrust deeper and deeper into her, Clara could feel her third orgasm building. She could feel the slimy appendages vying for space in her tiny, utterly filled cunt.

When all five tentacles momentarily stilled and then began pounding her pussy simultaneously, like one thick, monstrous cock, she couldn't take it anymore. The jackhammering of her stretched cunt by the massive girth of all the tentacles was driving her over the edge. With each rough thrust, Clara could feel the phallic tentacles just barely hitting her cervix, bottoming out her cunt.

She had never been pushed to the limit like this and she was loving the fucking and teasing of her body. The two tentacles in her ass began to slide in and out in rhythm as well, with a third pressing on her sphincter. It would slide in a bare inch or two and then completely out, so that Clara could feel her ass being stretched anew over and over even as it was getting fucked.

She could feel sharp pain in her clit and nipples, and looked down to see all three stretched as taut as they could go, the suckers on them twisting roughly to and fro. The sight of her own tits and pussy fucked made Clara moan, the depravity of it only making her more eager to come.

"It's pounding her like crazy, and her pussy is taking all of it! Look at that, just deeper and deeper... god, it's filling her up... fucking her ass and cunt like that at the same time. "

Knowing that this was all being watched, her body being penetrated in every possible way, her wet, full pussy on display, was intensely arousing for Clara. The tentacles working inside her sped up, splatters of sticky pussy juice sent flying by their roughness. It was the thought of coming again like this, with her every hole as full as possible and her legs spread so that every detail would be watched and recorded, that finally drove her over the edge.

With a muffled scream, Clara came again, her hardest yet. At the same time, something thick and hot flooded inside her. Torrents of ropy, frothy cum spilled out of her pussy past the writhing mass of tentacles still roughly fucking it, out of her stretched and stuffed asshole, and down her throat.

After it was finished, Clara hung there limp with shock. A dull haze seemed to settle over her mind, and she could only numbly feel the many violating tentacles slowly remove themselves from her abused orifices. Their motion elicited only the faintest moan, whether of protest or relief, she could not tell. The last thing she remembered was feeling like she was falling, before unconsciousness took her.

When Clara woke up, everything was pitch black. Her eyes felt filmy and crusted, and when she tried to reach up and rub them, her arms were stopped short by straps on her wrists. Irritated, she rolled her shoulder, struggling to rub the grainy feeling away. Wherever she was, it was full of hissing, beeping, and faint skritching noises. Clara groaned softly. She ached from head to foot, and a throbbing migraine pulsed behind her eyes.

The cause of the soreness in certain areas became increasingly clear as she began to recall the events preceding her blackout. Alone in the darkness, Clara blushed. She knew that she had been on god knows what kinds of crazy government drugs, first making her afraid, then making her aroused. She knew that her decision-making abilities had been compromised. She also knew that, at least in part, everything that had happened had fulfilled a fantasy of hers in one way or another.

Clara was overwhelmed by such a mix of conflicting feelings; it was rather hard to think clearly. She had been drugged and terrified out of her wits. The goons who had kidnapped her and were now holding her against her will would, in all likelihood, kill her at the end of all this. Uldra, as abjectly monstrous as it was, had offered a thread of hope.

Even the frailest filament felt like a blessing when you were hanging over an abyss. It was all just so... so confusing. Clara didn't want to feel like a victim, but this whole scenario was a nightmare. No matter how much she had enjoyed it in the moment, she knew she'd have never agreed to any of the insanity that had happened in that room if she hadn't been in such an awful, exceptional circumstance.

Clara felt like she was being unusually calm about the whole thing, actually. Didn't they say shock made you numb? It was amazing how detached one could be, contemplating the psychological ramifications of being abducted and basically forced into fucking a 3-story-tall alien spider monster. Could you even get Stockholm Syndrome for someone that wasn't your direct captor? Could you get it for something that wasn't even human?

Clara wrenched her thoughts away from that particular series of questions. She could have the luxury of being traumatized after escaping. Right now, falling apart wasn't an option, no matter how scary or insane things got. Clara squirmed, trying to feel out the cot she was on. Her ankles and wrists were bound, but maybe with a bit of wiggling...

Before Clara could even begin to attempt an escape, a crack of light appeared in the featureless blackness, silhouetting a figure. After a moment, lights flicked on, and Clara squinted painfully against the sterile fluorescent glare.

Chapter 3

"Ah! Our favorite little patient is awake."

A doctor, maybe in his mid-40s or so, strode across the room. To Clara's eyes, used to seeing the prematurely lined faces of other vagrants, he looked inappropriately young. The smooth skin of a 30-year-old, but the mature features of someone a decade older than that. His abnormally straight, gleaming teeth put her in mind of a white picket fence. The man had the flat eyes of a thing long dead. Walking roadkill. Clara hated the way he looked at her.

"I'm Dr. Sloan. You've been out for quite a while!"

He flipped casually through the clipboard attached to the foot of her bed, raising an eyebrow here and there.

"Four whole days, in fact. How do you feel?"

"Hungry."

Dr. Sloan laughed; a rich, buttery sound.

"I'm not surprised! You've been on IV nutrients this whole while, which don't exactly fill you up. Let's have those cuffs off, huh? And then we can get you something to eat, how does that sound?"

Clara's skin was crawling as the doctor, his hands unnaturally hot, undid the Velcro straps holding her to the bed. She rubbed her wrists absently, eying the older man askance. What the hell was his deal? Was this some kind of new tactic, trying to befriend her, make her cooperate?

Clara was surprised at how swiftly anger blossomed in her chest, even moreso when she realized that it was at least in part on Uldra's behalf. Though her relationship with the interplanetary horror was - well, Clara didn't even know if there was a word to describe it - but Uldra had been nicer and more honest to her than anyone else here had been since she got here.

Despite the, ah, very physical introduction the two had had, Uldra had actually asked for her permission. Hell, that was more than most bar creeps ever did. Her imprisonment, of course, complicated things. Did it count as coercion because she was trapped and threatened? It didn't feel that way.

Clara had no other word for it, but Uldra had seemed...nice. As nice as an alien monster could possibly be. She even kind of missed its weird, rhythmic voice echoing in her skull. The idea of the suits conspiring to win her over to manipulate Uldra somehow was infuriating.

Dr. Sloan continued to talk in what Clara was sure he imagined was a comforting manner, moving around the room to inspect various screens and instruments. She had been "very well taken care of", apparently, while she was out. There was something about his voice when he said it that made Clara sure he was wearing a smirk.

She silently flipped off his sterile white back as the doctor went on and on about just how graciously she had been treated, how carefully nursed. If what she remembered about the end of her tryst with Uldra was accurate, that had no doubt involved a bath at the very least. Clara repressed a shudder at the thought of the hot-handed doctor touching her unconscious, naked body. Somehow getting fucked by a tentacle-spider-alien was less disgusting to contemplate. Nothing for it now. At least she was clean.

Clara's hair was short again, too. It had been cut into a much neater version of the self-inflicted pixie style she normally wore. Clara reached up and ran a tentative hand through the caramel locks, the fluffy softness strange to her calloused fingers. Conditioner was not normally an aspect of her hygiene routine.

Only half-listening to Dr. Sloan, Clara took a good look at the room for the first time. It resembled that of any old hospital, complete with pale, sickly yellow walls and scuffed linoleum floors that squeaked underfoot. She recognized a heart monitor, but that was about it. Several other machines were displaying readouts, bleeping and clamoring for attention. Dr. Sloan had apparently been watching her careful tally of the equipment, as he offered some (downright condescending) explanation.

"Ahh, good eye. Those are your EEG readouts. Your brainwaves. Ever since you went under, activity in your cerebellum - the bottom bit of your brain - has been wild. That is very strange 'cause that generally suggests seizures and all kinds of other bad stuff, but here you are apparently fit as a fiddle!"

'Fit as a fiddle'? Is that how these fucking lunatics would describe me right now?

Clara tried not to let her disdain show too clearly, the patronizing tone Dr. Sloan was taking making her want to sink her nails into his stupid smiling face. It was like he was talking to a five-year-old. Wow, your brain do a weird thing! That mean bad stuff! Uh-ohhhh! Fuck off. Mutely, Clara accepted him shining a light into her eyes, measuring her pulse, and peering into her ears and down her throat.

A nurse briefly appeared, delivering a tray of food. Clara was pleasantly surprised to find that the unappetizing looking slurry was in fact somewhat watery but still tasty porridge with finely chopped bits of ham mixed in. She polished off the bowl and set to cleaning out the cup of yogurt, saving the apple for last.

Dr. Sloan was talking about something the whole time, the endless stream of words punctuated here and there with a hearty chuckle. Something about the dangers of lawn darts, lemonade, something something kids... Stupid suburban shit that Clara could not give a rat's left arsecheek about. The mundane delights of a home life were lost on her. She just nodded mutely along and ate her food, gnawing the fruit down to the seeds.

"Well, well! Healthy appetite on you, huh? That's promising. Alright, well, you seem in fine condition to me. I'll just have you cleared for discharge then, how does that sound? Buh-bye now!"

With a pat on the head, Dr. Sloan disappeared from the room. Clara spent a blissful few second imagining the sheet she was twisting in her hands was his pasty white neck.

Cleared for discharge, eh? She wasn't stupidly naïve enough to imagine that meant release from the facility entirely. No, Clara would probably be sent back to the old holding cells.

Her prediction proved right. Within the hour, Clara was given fresh scrubs and sent back into the general prisoner population. What friends she had made here inquired eagerly after her well-being and experiences. It was rare for someone to disappear for as long as she did and still make it back.

Clara found it surprisingly hard to lie, these being just about the only people here she felt she could trust at least a little. However, besides being embarrassingly intimate, the exact nature of the experiment she had survived had to be kept a secret for Uldra's sake. It would be no good if there were hidden microphones somewhere that picked up Clara describing the aliens true plan or degree of intelligence.

For the next two days, things returned to what Clara was grudgingly forced to think of as 'normal'. Wake up, eat, spend all day doing nothing, eat, sleep. She tried to keep busy catching up with the other prisoners, but it was hard to shake the lurking feeling of paranoia. The suits weren't done with her yet, not by a long shot. It didn't help that Clara was sure that cameras were dogging her steps. More than once she *caught the beady black gleam of the mechanical lens swiveling to lock onto her as soon as she entered a room.*

Some of the scientists who would come in to do occasional checkups would give Clara leering, meaningful looks that told her the events that had unfolded in that room were less than confidential. She smothered her embarrassment with anger, and made sure to be liberal with her scathing looks whenever she caught one of them ogling. All in all, being taken again was beginning to seem preferable to constantly being watched.

Time passed, and every morning, Clara waited to be called out again. There was no way these government squints would leave her alone now. Not when she was their only source of connection to their kidnapped alien. It was a little strange to think of Uldra that way, but it was truer for it than for Clara herself. She was at most a couple of thousand miles from home, not millions. Clara was proven correct in almost no time at all. On the fifth day, she was woken up and escorted from the communal holding cells by armed guards. Whether for protection for her or from her, Clara could not guess.

The same procedure as last time followed. Hosed down, given a stretchy white bodysuit, fitted with sensors, and strapped to a table. Clara could have sworn that the material used this time was thinner, more clinging. It lewdly outlined her pussy lips and nipples in a way that made her blush.

No injections, though. And, blessedly, there wasn't much of a wait time. Within minutes of the prep chamber clearing, Clara found herself sliding through down that familiar ol' shaft in the wall. She realized what she had been far too freaked out to notice last time - that the long 'commute' to Uldra's holding cell meant that the walls of that room were many meters thick. Just how strong did they think Uldra was...?

When Clara emerged, she craned her neck to better see what was going on. Things had drastically changed since the last time she was here. Uldra's egg was gone, for one. As far as she could see, not a single fragment remained. No doubt meticulously gathered and archived for testing. The nest of sensors and cables that had surrounded had also been cleared away somewhat. And then there was Uldra itself.

The alien had not retreated into another cocoon, but nor was it still active and mobile. It appeared to have sort of folded up, its abdomen raised above its head (which was down close to the floor) and its legs drawn up to its body.

The six gleaming black appendages had stiffened and arranged themselves almost like a tripod... a hexpod? The legs were clearly braced in a way that supported the gargantuan mass of Uldra's thorax in its unusual position. Most noticeable was the glow. Inside the glassy black mass of its bulbous oval abdomen a brilliant light shifted and pulsed. It looked almost like the aurora, green shot with threads of blue, pink, and purple.

Clara couldn't deny that it looked mesmerizingly beautiful. A truly alien light show. She watched, awed, for several long minutes. Was it just the machines, or was the alien being emitting a low hum of its own? The longer she stared at the scintillating light, the more Clara was convinced that she could almost read a pattern in it. Like morse code, or lighthouse signals... She strove to perceive the meaning, but it was like trying to find purchase on slick glass.

Tentatively, Clara reached out in her mind. She was shocked, and surprised at her shock, that there was no response. What else was there to do? Her only communication with Uldra had been telepathic, and it's not like Clara had any innate abilities to initiate it herself.

What if she had imagined it all? Uldra had only 'spoken' when Clara had been pumped full of fear drugs and hallucinogens. After that wore off, she hadn't heard the aliens voice again. Clara fought the sinking feeling in her stomach. She had to believe that there was some chance of escape, or she would go mad.

"-V-19, can you hear us?"

Clara jerked her attention away from her brooding thoughts. The intercom had crackled to life. Looks like the experiment of the day was beginning. Clara briefly entertained thoughts of mulish non-compliance, but she didn't feel like pressing her luck too much. If the escape plan was still in the cards... and it is, she thought stubbornly... then it would be best to just keep her head down and not give them undue cause to doubt her word. She was, after all, still covering for Uldra's lack of sentience.

Clearing her throat, Clara responded with an affirmative. She had expected more questions, perhaps about what she saw or felt. Instructions, maybe, to try and communicate with Uldra. Instead, there were several long minutes of silence. What she didn't expect was a soft crackle near her ear, and the voice from the intercom murmuring next to her.

"Hello, C-V-19. Comfortable? I hope so."

Clara didn't react, her eyes roving the blank walls, and the voice laughed.

"I know you can hear me. I had this little comm installed after your last performance with the monster. None of the other researchers know about it... or about the extra cameras I had mounted. All pointed at that sweet little pussy of yours, and those perky little tits. You see, after last time, I enjoyed the recording of you getting fucked over and over. It was incredible, watching your pussy get filled with alien cum.

So this time, I thought I'd get a private little show. I'll be watching everything, and the video will be saved for me to use whenever I want... Just like that creature is about to use your body."

Heart beating, Clara had to clench her teeth tightly to avoid swearing or screaming. No doubt giving the pervert away would result in all kinds of unpleasant negative consequences. She would have to endure it for now. Surely... surely Uldra would save them both. It couldn't have all been in her head... But what was this creep talking about? Uldra seemed to have fallen into a suspended animation state once more.

"I'm sure you're wondering how that's gonna happen... well... I had a few theories, and my colleagues... well. They were as eager to approve my suggestions as I was to see them used. In the end, even if that alien thing doesn't react, we're still gonna get a performance from you. Heh, heh, heh..."

There was a sudden hum from under the table. A myriad of articulated arms unfolded from underneath, poised over Clara much like Uldra had been. They worked in a flurry, and soon Clara was quivering naked in the cool air. The mechanical grippers had shredded her clothes with swift efficiency.

Chapter 4

Suddenly, the captive had a good idea of what kind of 'suggestions' she was about to experience. Clara expected another dose of aphrodisiac, and was surprised when instead two metal claws descended and clamped down on her breasts. The steel digits squeezed like a vise, pale flesh protruding between them. Clara winced, biting her tongue.

The claws had some kind of holes in the middle that her nipples had been pulled into by a strong suction. Clara could see them, red and puffy, in the clear tube portion of the machine. Cold metal brushed her thighs and she flinched away, but there was nothing she could do. Two braces, shaped like brackets, inserted themselves between her pussy lips and spread wide. Clara's pussy was utterly exposed.

She had resisted making a noise before, but she couldn't help crying out when she felt a painful pinch and then a powerful pull on her clit. Looking between her legs, she could see a tube latched on to the sensitive organ. It was digging into her flesh with sharp, tiny claws, sealing itself to her clit - which, too, was visible. The vacuum inside had sucked it right into the transparent duct, forcing it to engorge with blood.

"I thought that an intravenous delivery system just wasn't good enough, so I created this instead. It doesn't serve any purpose other than to humiliate and excite you. Not that any of the other researchers wanted to point that out. I think we all wanted to see you tortured and punished in some novel ways..."

Clara didn't understand what the guy was talking about at first, until suddenly - she screamed. Sharp needles had extended from inside the suction tubes and pierced her artificially swollen nipples and clit. A cold rush of injection spread from them, flooding into her body. They didn't retract, either. Instead, the serum slowly dripped into Clara's body, designed to keep her at unnatural maximum arousal for as long as possible. At first, Clara had to clench her teeth and squeeze her eyes shut, struggling not to cry from the pain. But slowly, as the chemicals took hold, the agony morphed into pleasure. Not that the pain was any less, but now each throb sent shocks of ecstasy through her pussy and tits.

"Ah, I can see it's starting to take effect. Can you feel your little cunt getting wet yet? No use denying it. I can see all your vital readings right in front of me. You're excited, aren't you? Well, don't worry, it's just beginning. The others thought this was an automated program, but I'm controlling everything from here. I decide what happens to you now."

The scientist spoke in a husky, breathy voice. Clara could imagine him already jerking off to her body, disgusting. It was hard to focus on her anger with the aphrodisiac in her system, so Clara was forced to file away her fantasies of revenge for when she regained control of her mind and body. As she watched, more robotic limbs revealed themselves.

"How about this? You took all those thick tentacles so well last time. A practiced slut like you doesn't need a warm up, does she?"

"Unnnghaa! Ahh!"

Without warning, something thick and hard plunged into Clara's tight cunt, and she cried out in involuntary delight. The painful stretching of her unprepared pussy was transformed into nothing but pleasure. The level of chemicals inside Clara was reaching levels that made it impossible to form coherent thoughts. All she could comprehend was a need to be filled and fucked. The mechanical cock was rigid and covered in metal studs.

The protrusions weren't perfectly smooth bumps, but in fact had slight points. Instead of sliding into her dripping cunt smoothly, they caught painfully on the way in.

Each time the appendage slid out and then rammed back in, Clara moaned. The inward thrust felt like it was going to tear her pussy right in half, and she loved it.

"That's right... moan nice and loud... There's a good slut, with a greedy little cunt."

To her disappointment, the needles in her clit and nipples retracted. However, that didn't last long. Suddenly, they pierced the swollen and sensitive flesh once again. Over and over, stimulating and injecting Clara with more aphrodisiac.

"Unnhh, yes... oh, it hurts... more...!"

The cock in her pussy suddenly began to lengthen, telescoping until Clara could feel metal studs slamming into her cervix. The agony should have been debilitating, but instead she moaned and thrashed with orgasm. The suction on her nipples increased, and the swollen nubs were pulled almost a full inch into the tubes attached to them.

"More, huh? You really are a naughty little minx, aren't you? How I'd love to pump my cum deep inside you... watch it drip out of your pussy after I punish and play with it for hours... Maybe I'll get you pulled aside for some special experiments. Test the limits of your body. Like, for example, how much of my thick semen I can get inside you..."

Panting and glistening with sweat, Clara managed a laugh. Somehow, in spite of her delirious state, she still managed to find this talk utterly ridiculous. Pathetic, human ego.

"Haha... ah... Uldra... you can't... nhh, ahh! Can't compare...!"

"Uldra? What...? Is that your little pet name for that fucking abomination? You fucking bitch, I'll-"

Before Clara could find out just what the enraged freak was going to do, an alarm blared. The intercom hissed to life.

The words coming out of it sounded garbled, meaningless to Clara, who was still trapped in a haze. Lights flashed, and there was horrible noise like a thousand windows being smashed at once. Everything seemed to shake, and-

The machinery surrounding Clara was suddenly ripped away. Uldra had emerged.

Effortlessly, the massive alien batted away the offending mechanism with a flick of its thickly armored leg. Clara looked up at the towering mass of the alien without comprehension, aware only of the loss of the sexual stimulus she had been forced to crave.

Uldra had changed in the time since their last encounter. No longer was it smoothly obsidian black. It looked almost as though it were made out of alexandrite now, the sleek armored carapace covered in glittering, gemlike protrusions.

It was like a geode had been cracked open and brought to life. The crystalline structures glittered with deep purples and greens. Uldra's shape had changed somewhat, too, becoming more elongated, low-slung, and predatory.

All of this was no doubt of deep interest to the scientists, but to Clara, nothing meant anything anymore. Freed of the restraints, she lay there without even trying to move or escape. Reaching down, Uldra gathered her close to its body with its smaller graspers. Clara was limp in their hold and aware only of a pleasant warmth. Uldra had slid back the armored plates on its belly, revealing its soft and velvety underside.

Uldra had spent its time in stasis adapting, using the genetic and psychic information gathered from Clara to tailor itself both to earth's atmosphere and to its new mate. Everything about it was now ideally suited precisely to Clara and her body.

Tentacles wrapped around her wrists and ankles, and pulled them taut. Her limbs disappeared to the knees and elbows into muscular pockets that held her gently but firmly in place. She was immobilized, spread eagled and nude. Clara writhed slowly, the satin warmth delightful against her ultra-sensitive skin.

"Clara you are being manipulated? Can you hear me?" Uldra questioned.

The voice in her head was deep, resounding, like a tolling bell. Clara couldn't react, only faint surprise suffusing her awareness. The excessive dose of arousing chemicals she had received had not had time to fade from her.

"I see you are not clear in your mind or body. I will help and give you what you need and crave and then free us both"

None of the words made any sense to Clara, for whom the aching need in her pussy was the only issue she could focus on. Fortunately for her, that was about to be well taken care of.

"Look! It's getting ready to mate with her again! Focus cameras 4, 6, 7, 11, and 16. Make sure everything is operating. Are the microphones balanced? The beast must have been unable to resist the pheromones she was putting out. It looks so different now. Perhaps a different stage of its maturity, like a molt? I bet it'll have some new tricks for her..."

Though the experimenters were wrong in their premise, the conclusion was correct. Uldra had changed very deliberately, not as a result of some innate process, but it definitely was planning something special for Clara. The tentacles that began to probe her body were quite different in shape and structure than before.

There were four kinds now, all with their own purpose. There were pencil-thin ones with heads that opened like flowers, revealing toothed petals and dozens of wriggling cilia.

Slightly thicker ones, about as big around as a human finger, that were covered in ridges and studs. Even thicker ones, about as big as the average human cock, with heads that split into six smaller, writhing tendrils. The last were the thickest. As big around as a wrist, with bulbous heads, these tentacles had large swellings every few inches. All of them glistened with thick, clear slime.

Chapter 5

As they roamed over Clara's body, the substance left her skin shining and slick.

"Unnh... inside... need more... inside me..."

Clara's nipples were a bright red, painfully erect and long from their session in the suction tubes. Angry lines showed where the metal claws had sunk into the flesh of her breasts. Two of the thinnest tendrils approached them, flicking and teasing Clara's abused nipples. She moaned, thrusting her tits out eagerly.

There was a sudden crack, and Clara howled. Uldra had used the tentacles like a whip, leaving a welt across her free-hanging and exposed tits that neatly crossed both nipples. Crack, crack, crack! They bounced with every strike, and Clara arced. She was struggling to push her breasts out further, accepting each precisely-placed blow with gasps and moans.

"God, she's loving it. Look at the slut, you can see she's practically about to cum. Get a still shot of that, with the stripes right across her tits."

The tendrils opened up and clamped down on Clara's pert breasts, their toothed insides providing the perfect mix of pain and pleasure Clara so desperately needed. The cilia within massaged, stroked, pulled, and squeezed the puffy pink nipples. Clara could only moan louder, thick juice dripping down her pussy lips. The arrhythmic twisting and pinching was already bringing her close to orgasm. Uldra was a thousand times better than any inert machine possible could be.

"Look at how wet she is, zoom in. I think there's something in the slime its secreting that makes her even more receptive to its tentacles."

"Ahhh... ah... ah- ohh! Unhh, it hurtsss... hurts so good... Please, more... fill me up..."

"Listen to her beg! She's too horny to think straight, trying to talk to that thing as if it can understand her. Not like it matters, looks like she's about to get what she wants anyway... Switch to camera 6 and get in nice and close on her wet slit."

A tentacle of middling thickness probed her pussy, wriggling inside. It penetrated deep into her cunt, the muscular tendrils at the end stroking her cervix. They were coated in a relaxant, stroking and massaging. Clara moaned. She could feel the penetrating, flexible digits forcing their way deeper into her than anything had ever been. They were pushing their way into her womb, slithering inside and filling her completely.

In and out, fucking her faster and faster. Clara had never imagined her pussy could be stuffed like this. The flexing, throbbing tentacle had forced its way past her cervix and deep into her body, and there was even a visible bulge on her belly when it was all the way inside her.

The thought of the slimy, muscular organ violating her in a way no human possibly could was intensely arousing. Crying out, Clara's pussy clamped down as she came, panting and twitching. She was, however, far from satisfied. It seemed that Uldra knew that, and had no plans of stopping its assault on her body any time soon.

As the tentacle slid out, one of the ridged and studded tendrils wrapped around it in a spiral. When the entwined tentacles pushed their way into Clara's tight pussy again, she gasped.

"Ahh! Yes, oh... ahh! Uahh!"

Every thrust came harder and harder, and went deeper and deeper. Clara cried out each time, pussy juice mingling with the slime Uldra was secreting and coating her thighs. The ridges, so varied and ever so slightly flexible - like hard rubber - felt incredible. Once again, Clara felt like her pussy was being torn in half, and she received each hard thrust with a delighted moan.

The pleasurable pain was twofold - first, the ridges catching on her opening, and second, the more intense and unique pain of the studs pushing past her cervix. It seemed like every inch of her aching cunt was being abused and teased. The tendrils clamped on Clara's nipples suckled rhythmically, their thorned insides digging into the swollen and sensitive flesh.

Every once in a while, they would twist or pull sharply, making Clara moan with pained delight. She imagined it was like her body was being milked, her body rendered immobile and subjected to pleasure and humiliation entirely outside her control. She came again, but this time Uldra didn't stop. Another ridged tendril wound inside her, and then yet another. Each of them squirmed in deeper and deeper, disregarding Clara's breathless pleading for reprieve.

"It's starting to stretch her cunt again just like last time. Those textured appendages must be tearing her pussy apart, and she's loving it... Listen to that moaning. That's the sound of a slut being fucked the way she deserves."

The idea of her violation being watched was intensely arousing, and Clara tried to spread her legs and expose herself further. Every word she said was contradicted by her attempts to ensure that every moment of her pussy getting fucked was as visible as possible.

"Nnn... no... D-don't stretch my pussy... in front of them... ahh, ah! It feels so good! My little cunt being punished for t-their enter-... nnhh, entertainment... My wet... little hole is s-so sore... More... fill it up more... while they watch..."

"Oh, so she likes being fucked for us. Helpless little slut, having her sopping cunt stretched till it can't take anymore... Zoom in and get some stills. Hear that, little slut? Every second of your eager young pussy getting punished is being recorded. Every moan, every time you come from being fucked and used."

Even as the voice spoke, Clara came again. Waves of pleasure wracked her body, heightened by the knowledge that her twitching pussy was being filmed. Groaning, it was a few moments before she was aware of the tentacles retreating. A new pressure at her entrance signaled the presence of the thickest of the tendrils.

Simultaneously, one of the grasping tendrils latched on to Clara's engorged clit. She hadn't even been aware of how much it ached to be played with, and she spasmed with pleasure. The toothed appendage twisted and pulled on her clit, easily bringing Clara to another orgasm. More thin, ropy tentacles looped around her breasts, squeezing them. The rush of blood into her nipples brought freshly heightened sensation. Before the last twinges of Clara's orgasm had faded, she felt the thick head of the huge tentacle begin to force its way inside.

"Uuaahh... it's too big! Nnn... nno... Oh, ah... it's so thick, it's not gonna fit... inside me... Nno! Ah! Oh god, unhhh, it hurts, it's stretching me...! My little cunt is gonna tear!"

"That thing is huge... I can't believe it's going inside that tight little hole of hers... and look, it's not done..."

Even as the massive tentacle slowly penetrated Clara's quivering cunt, one of the mid-sized tentacles began to probe her ass. The massive bulb of the thickest tentacle suddenly slid into her pussy with a squelch, and the tendril at her ass penetrated her simultaneously. The thick slime coating it made it easy. Clara writhed, moaning and begging - not for the tentacles to stop, but for more. The thick length in her pussy obligingly pressed onward. The swell of one of the bulges slowly began to penetrate her.

With the unusual shape of this tentacle, Clara would never have any rest. Every other inch, another exceptionally thick protrusion would stretch her pussy anew. Two, then three of the knots disappeared into her dripping cunt. Then Clara felt them press against her cervix.

"N-no! Unn, my pussy can't take it...! Not all the way in, n- Ahhh!"

The head of the monstrously girthy tentacle penetrated her womb. Clara had never felt so incredibly full, but her limits were tested further as the tentacle in her ass slid forward another few inches. Despite her protests, a second one of the same size joined it, pushing its way into her ass and joining the one already there.

They writhed in deeper, further than any cock or toy possibly could, until a good 15 inches had disappeared inside her. When the bulbous tentacle in Clara's pussy bottomed out and began to slide out, she moaned anew. She could only take two more such complete journeys, each a little faster than the other, before she came again. Still there was no rest. As the tentacle head pushed inside her again, her cunt pulsed and twitched.

Clara was gleaming with sweat and slime, but still not entirely satisfied. Her mind had cleared somewhat, but the numbing arousal of the chemical cocktail was being replaced by the deep and burning pleasure of natural desire augmented by Uldra's own secretions. Clara needed more, head lolling with lust as the tentacles milked and suckled her breasts and clit. The tentacles in her ass slid out, leaving her feeling strangely empty, but were quickly replaced.

"Oh no, no... my pussy could barely take it... nnoo!"

A bulging tentacle pressed insistently at her ass, harder and harder until it suddenly slid inside with a pained cry from Clara. A toy of this size would have been inflexible, impossible to force in much further. But Uldra was no toy. The knotted tentacle writhed in deeper, eliciting more pained cries from Clara. Every part of her body was being used and tortured now. Puffy, aching nipples and clit being pulled and twisted, pussy and even womb utterly filled, and now her ass being penetrated with no way to stop it.

"Fuck, just look at that. Dripping holes being stuffed and fucked. The aphrodisiac must have worn off by now, but she's still loving it. Just a natural slut, then, who knows she deserves to have all her holes stretched and used. Get a good shot of it fucking her ass and pussy at the same time. It'll go well with the audio of her begging for more..."

Clara moaned, knowing her body was being filmed and exposed for the pleasure of a bunch of perverts, but she couldn't help being excited by that. As the bulging tentacle in her pussy slid out, studded tendrils wound around it, adding a new layer of pain to the next penetration. Each bulging knot, wrapped with undulating studs, elicited pained gasps from the bound and helpless Clara.

"Ahh! Oh, my pussy... it's on fire... I feel so full and s-stretch, nnhh, please... I can't come anymore... Nnh, it hurts, nghh, don't-! Ah!"

Another studded tendril plunged into her pussy, followed by one forcing itself into her ass. Her holes felt like they couldn't possibly take any more abuse, yet Uldra showed no sign of letting up. Her nipples were pulled taut, twisted sharply, and Clara came again. Her body was still shaking with pleasure when one of the cock-sized tentacles plunged into her mouth.

The numbing secretion it produced allowed it to slide effortlessly down her throat, effectively gagging her. Clara was reduced to muffled moans and gasps, unable to even plead for the assault on her body to stop. It seemed there was one final punishment left for her to endure.

Two more ridged tentacles, thin but unique in their texture, squirmed into her ass, and... Clara bucked, the high pitched keen stifled by the tentacle in her throat. One of the cock-sized tentacles was probing her pussy. There was no way. No way. And yet, the thick, clear slime coating it seemed to have enough relaxant property to make it possible.

The grasping tendrils at its head squirmed and pried at her opening, which was tightly clamped atop the tentacles already stuffed inside her wet hole. Little by little, it pushed its way in. Clara moaned and writhed, but was unable to escape the slow and inevitable thrust into her body. Inch by inch, the tentacle made its way inside her, until it too was buried all the way in her womb.

Clara's stomach was distended by the mass of tentacles fucking her pussy and forcing their way past her cervix. Her ass throbbed and clenched on the appendages stretching it. In total, she had one thick and bulbous tentacle in both her ass and pussy, one cock-sized one in her pussy, and 3 studded finger-sized ones in her both her ass and pussy. Not to mention the one filling her throat. All of them now properly placed, they began to fuck Clara's holes mercilessly and rhythmically. When the ones in her ass slid out, the ones in her pussy slid in, meaning she didn't have a second of rest from the pain and pleasure assaulting her senses.

"It's amazing, what she can take. A real champion of a cockslut, huh? Make sure you get that in HD, her pussy dripping with juice from getting fucked by a monster's cocks.

She'd probably let it fuck her till she died, the little whore, as long as it filled up her cunt and ass. Listen to those moans. She's loving it, loving being put on display as she gets punished and stretched."

Faster and faster, harder and harder. Clara moaned wildly, imagining how it must look. Legs parted, her stuffed holes on display getting pounded. Tits and clit being milked and sucked. Throat being fucked so that all she could do was moan. As the orgasm mounted, the tentacles inside her began to throb in a strange, new way.

Suddenly, something thick and hot exploded insider her pussy, ass, and down her throat. Other tentacles, poised over her body, poured rivers of sticky cum over her body. The substance shot out of her pussy and ass with every thrust, filling her to the brim. Clara's scream was muffled as she came, this orgasm longer and more intense than any before.

The pleasure reached its climax, Clara knew there's absolute nothing the alien would do to get them out of the place.

She just wanted more and more of the encounter. This is way more soothing to her.

For the first time after long months, she was happy she has encounters with the alien. Clara once more found herself falling into blackness, and was aware of nothing more but she hopes for more of the sex with the alien.

THE END

Description

Rick a professional firefighter who loves his job so much. Although he'd been involved in a few events he was not proud of, he turned his life around. When he got invited to a party by his girlfriend and blackmailed into something that started as a game. He was looking for a reason to live, and he found it in Flora. Sexy, smart and determined to show Ricky that she was ready for a serious relationship. Ricky will stop at nothing to make the relationship work. They fall in love and lost focus on everyone else.

Chapter 1

Box alarm, one-zero-four-seven. Three engines and a ladder from the five- nine- nine responding. Rick's time off had reached. Granted "on time" the moment he sat down for his meal at the station house. This fighting job was the only woman he could ask for.

The engine co.19 turned the corner with siren and lights going. Rick glanced outside at the moving traffic. His colleagues were seated two forward facing, two rear. Rick stared out the open window, the cold window, the cold wind blew his dark hair back, his eyes focusing on nothing. His knees brushed the gear every time the engine bumped over sewer access panels or potholes.

They were at the scene, the old upper fixer house was an old shell of its former self. There were broken glass panes, rotting beams and blown rooftops. The blaze had reduced everything to the ground, smoke wafted up into the air and was carried away by the wind. His boots hit the ground. It was time to do what he did best. Save lives...

*****

"Shit," Flora muttered as she got off the plane. She was used to hangovers especially in college but not like this one. Her head hurt so horribly and she couldn't feel her legs. She'd fallen asleep on the plane and the attendant had to wake her up.

She dragged her backpack over her shoulder which sent more pain to her back. She had stayed out until two A.M laughing notoriously to everything about her life. The bright light hit her face as she walked through the airport. The airport was full as she trudged ahead. Her head was filled with nothing but bad thoughts. How was she going to survive the next few days? Would her mother expect her to talk to her after what she did to her?

She stepped onto the escalator leading down to the baggage carousels and the movement made her retch. She quickly fumbled in her bag for a tissue and held it to her mouth. She never noticed the watching crowd at the bottom as she descended the escalator because she had a tissue in her mouth and her eyes were closed.

When she stepped off, she nearly fell on top of a man with a paunch and not much hair.

"Pardon me," she said in a voice as husky as her brain was feeling.

The man looked up at her as his face softened.

"Anytime," he said as he stepped aside. She walked briskly to the exit and waited for a taxi. Everyone was being picked but not her. She hated the attention from her family, surprising them would be a great idea. They were expecting her but not today. All she wanted was to attend her father's funeral and get back to her life.

She ran her fingers through her hair, twirling her curls around her index finger. She was only twenty-eight years old yet she looked younger than her age. She was beautiful with long lashes, perfect and natural blond hair and bright blue eyes thanks to her mother's genes.

She squinted at the taxi window as the driver pulled up. She was not desperate to get home. The taxi driver helped her put her bag in the trunk and they sped off.

"Well, well, well, look who's back."

Flora set a plate of baked sweet potatoes on the table then looked into the eyes of her childhood enemy.

Angie Brooks. Angie had been a thorn on her side ever since they were born. She was a rock in her shoe and a colossal pain in the ass. Angie was always one step ahead every time she turned around. Angie was faster and better in games.

They never acted like cousins; they were sworn enemies. In the seventh grade, Angie had beaten her out for head cheerleader and caught her at the drive in with her childhood crash. A girl never forgets something like that.

"Angie Brooks," she said. She hated to admit to herself that except for the hair, her cousin was still pretty.

"Nice to meet you." Angie grabbed one potato and stuffed it in her mouth. "I have a boyfriend now and we are getting married soon."

Flora forced a smile on her lips. "Just great," she told herself. She never cared about her or her random boyfriends but she'd entertained the thought and fantasy of Romeo and Juliet ending for her cousin and her loser boyfriends.

"Are you married?" Angie asked.

"No."

Angie gave her a look filled with pity.

"Are you dating someone?" she asked curiously.

"No, I'm single as always," Flora said in a defensive tone.

"I bet you are still a virgin as always," Angie concluded. Flora fought the urge to shove the potatoes up Angie's nose.

"So, I hear you decided to disown your mother."

"I haven't done such a thing."

"Oh," Angie reached for another potato and scooted down the line. "I must not have heard correctly." Flora doubted there was anything wrong with Angie's hearing. She wished she could slap some protein pack on Angie's fizzy hair. Her gazed looked through the living room filled with people, some she didn't recognize. She located her mother, her blond hair was in perfect order, her make up flawless. She resembled her mother. At forty-six, she looked young and could pass for thirty.

"You finally came back, I thought you were dead." Her attention was drawn to Mrs. Owen. She looked the same as

Flora remembered. She couldn't recall her name though. Everyone had always referred to her as Mrs. Owen.

"Can I help you with something to eat?" Flora asked politely. She offered Flora her plate as she snagged an egg. "Some of that please."

"Would you like some potatoes too?"

"Makes me gassy and bloated."

Flora frowned. "Never mind." She shouldn't have tried. She sat Mrs. Owen at the table then headed to the bar. She had forgotten the after-funeral ritual of gathering and talking while dining with relatives. She didn't feel comfortable in the least, all she wanted was to leave. She was on display. Everyone thought she abandoned her parents. She'd never been outgoing like her cousin. She poured herself some bourbon and sipped as she watched from a far.

Flora knew she was sometimes compulsive, she only had one addiction. She loved reading, her taste in reading leaned towards self Jo-help books mostly because she wanted to learn how to conquer a man. She was about to exit the bar when a stranger tapped her shoulder.

"Hi," she tried to remember if she knew him.

"Don't try so hard. I'm Ricky." The gentleman stretched out his hand for a handshake.

"Are we related?" She tried to sound polite.

"I can tell that you are not so social. I'm....."

"He is Ricky, my boyfriend's brother." Angie interjected before Ricky could finish. Angie and Ricky shook their collective heads and drank their scotch. Flora looked at the tall handsome guy and faked a smile. She never wanted to get involved or socialize with anyone Angie knew.

"I'm sorry but I have to leave, my mother needs me." Flora lied. There was a pause in their conversation before Angie said. "Did I miss something?"

"No, everything's fine," Ricky answered.

"If you may excuse me." Flora walked to her mother. They both concurred with a mutual nod as Flora disappeared. Ricky turned to look at Angie with a stunned face.

"Why would you lie about who I am?" Ricky asked.

"I'm sorry but I had to lie." Angie defended herself.

"She will think I'm a liar when she finds out that I'm your boyfriend," Ricky replied.

"I have a plan, that's why I lied."

"I thought we came for a funeral not to lie about who we are." He tried to walk away but Angie held him by the arm.

"You are a professional firefighter, since when did you start having empathy to strangers?" She tried to lower her voice.

"You want me to lie and steal?" Ricky was shocked. "And don't call them strangers, they are victims."

"I will tell you later, for now just pretend to be my future brother-in-law. You must earn her trust." She faked to smile to the nosy crowd.

"How will I do that within these few days?" Ricky scanned the room if anybody was eavesdropping.

"I don't know, figure something out." She patted him on the back. "I don't know her and you never gave me a heads up."

"Now you know her, I need a refill." Angie shrugged pointing to the shelves at the bar. Reluctantly, Ricky walked to the bar to get her the drink she wanted.

Chapter 2

"Flora honey, you are not eating enough since you got here. What you are eating is not enough to keep a woman alive," Mrs. McAllister said, then seemed to think that was the funniest joke she would ever say.

"Keep a woman alive and Ricky here is an expert in women's health. He is a health and fitness coach." Betty McAllister replied as she nearly exploded in adoring laughter at her own witticism. She stared at her mother. Ricky sensed the tension between them.

They were sitting at the dining table.

"Mum," Flora said loudly so she could be heard over their self-induced chuckles. "I'm leaving today, you buried daddy a day before the planned date. I guess I have nothing left to do here. If you need someone to keep you company, I'm sure Angie and her friends will be suitable." She said loudly while pointing to Ricky, who'd just poured himself more wine from the jug but hadn't offered to refill her glass.

The stare made Betty put her hand over her mouth to hide her mirth. "You wanna tell me how you two met before today?"

"No!" Flora and Ricky said in unison, then refused to stare at one another.

"I want you to stay for a while."

"Mum," Flora said firmly, "I wanna know why you want me to stay."

"Honey," Betty replied as she reached for her hand, but Flora moved to pick her wine glass.

"Do you need a refill?" Ricky asked when he saw her grimace.

She looked at him then back to her mother, "I need to leave and don't pretend like we are buddies."

"You need to stay until they read your father's will." She placed her wine glass gently on the table.

"Uh," Flora said and she instantly sobered. "I don't think he would leave me anything after you poisoned him against me." Her voice was soft as though she regretted something. "But that's great with me, I don't need anything from anyone. I can work my ass off." She said leaning a bit forward and for the first time, she felt like there was life inside her body.

"You have to respect your father's last wish," Ricky said loudly.

"No one asked for your opinion." She fairly hissed at him, then turned back to her mother.

"The two of you should not spit at each other in front of me," Betty murmured, her face looked as though she wanted to throw a party. "You two can talk about your lives."

The last thing Flora wanted was to tell the scowling raven in front of her all about her uneventful life. When she stood up, she staggered a bit, "I need to rest or I can just jump in the mouth of the nearest dog outside."

"You two are alike more than you know. I like your sense of humor." He stood up and took her arm. He looked at her in a way that made Flora hope that she wasn't going to bury her face on his chest. She didn't think she had the strength to fight him off.

Still stumbling, she followed him to her room, he showed her the bed, she didn't think about the lack of privacy. She just fell into her bed and went to sleep, there was a smile on her face because she thought that the worst day of her life was over. She was so wrong.

Two days after the burial, Flora McAllister woke up late and narrowly escaped meeting with her best friend from high school. The two had plans to meet at Westfield Ohio's bar for a night of margaritas and gossip.

But her mother had different plans for her.

"I'd like you to stay for the reading of the will," Betty said as soon as Flora walked into the living room. A slight wrinkle furrowed her brow at her mother's comment. Flora would rather chew on cud than getting sucked to attend the reading of the will. After all, her father made it clear that he wasn't going to leave her anything.

"I have plans now." She lied and spread butter onto her toasted bread. She was approaching thirty and could not forgive her mother for cheating on her father several times and making out with her friend from high school.

"I know you hate me but I'm a changed person now." Betty remarked, softly.

"Good for you. I don't hate you."

Flora packed her suitcase and looked around her room one last time. Nothing had changed since the day she left. Her wallpapers were still intact and her music collections were just the way she left them. It's like her parents knew she'd be back. Her things had been kept waiting for her. Instead of feeling welcomed, the room felt oppressive just like her mother. She had to leave.

All she had to do was listen to the will and say goodbye. She wouldn't be surprised if her father left everything to her mother and Angie. She wasn't looking forward to the confrontations. She left her room and headed downstairs to her father's office for the reading of the will.

She was welcomed by a greeting from her longtime friend at the entrance of the office.

"Good morning, Miss McAllister," he said as she walked into the room. Paul Shaw, her father's estate lawyer sat behind a huge mahogany desk and looked up as she walked in. She stretched out her hand and greeted him before sitting down beside her mother.

"Is everyone present?" he asked looking at the empty seat across him.

"We are all present," Angie said circling the cross necklace on her neck.

"Thanks you all for coming," Paul cleared his throat, "To make things short, I would appreciate if you kept your opinions and questions until I'm done." He squared the documents in front of him and began with his speech. "I, Brock McAllister, resident of Westfield, state of Ohio, do declare that this is my last will and testament therefore revoking all the wills in the past. I nominate and appoint my friend Paul Shaw to execute this will."

Flora listened with half an ear as Paul read the duties of the executor. She didn't care about the duties. Her mind was filled with other things. She scanned the room but Ricky was nowhere to be seen.

Could he have left? she asked herself.

The tension that filled the room was almost tangible. A few seconds later, Ricky entered the room and sat on the empty chair next to her, the clean scent of his after shave teased her nose. Paul paused for a minute but Betty motioned him to continue.

Ricky's hand brushed hers as he placed his arm on his chair. His shirt touched her bare skin, she tried to stay still like nothing happened. Paul paused and Flora returned her gaze to him. She watched Paul set each read page aside.

"To my wife Betty, I will always love you and thank you for the daughter you gave me. I hereby leave her all the unexpired insurance." Everyone listened carefully as he read on.

"To my daughter, Flora McAllister, I give all my tangible properties and my estate under the condition that she gets married. If she refuses to comply with the terms of this will, the properties and estates referred to in this will should be given to the state of Ohio.”

Flora felt rigid on her chair, heat flushed her face and her heart was racing.

It was too much to take in. She was too confused to listen. What changed her father’s mind about her? She replayed the last part in her mind. How can he force her to settle down?

That was like a slap to her face. Paul finished and looked up from the will. There was silence in the office. No one wanted to speak first. Betty asked the question that was on everybody’s mind.

“Where is the original will?”

“This is the only will. Brock changed his will before he got a heart attack,” Paul replied.

“What do you mean heart attack? My mom told me he died of natural causes.” Flora scoffed, trying her best to forget about the will.

“He died of heart attack. Your mother can confirm it.” Flora stared at her mother, who was crying.

“Forget it, I’m done with this family.” Flora stood. She wasn’t about to let her father control her from the grave. “I’ll leave the inheritance to the state.”

“You can’t give the state what you don’t have, until you accept the terms.”

“You can contest the will if you have grounds, like lack of mental capacity.” Paul confirmed.

“There it is.” Flora stood up, lifting her hands up. “My father was crazy and out of his mind.”

Betty stood up and held Flora by the arm. “Honey, this is what your father wanted, you don’t have to rebel all the time.”

“Honey!” Flora removed strands of fly away hair from her mouth. “You can’t call me honey after everything you did to me and dad. I always sat on my bed till late waiting for my mother to come back and read me a story while you were out partying with your boyfriends, and don't get me started on how you denied me several times that I'm not your daughter in front of your boyfriends. You always said that I was the daughter of my dad's first wife, who never existed."

Flora's stomach twitched, tears rolled over her cheeks as she tried to let go of Betty's hand. Betty's grip was too tight.

There was silence in the room.

"I'm sorry, honey," Betty apologized.

"All you ever cared about was dad's money. I'm sure dad found out about your infidelity and that's why he got a heart attack. I always blamed dad for not standing up for me. He adored you and did everything you said." Flora turned her hard gaze to the lawyer. "He even threw me out because you told him to. I was your child, for Pete's sake, why would you treat me like garbage?"

Flora tried to stand firm on her weak knees. She forced herself despite the fear and pain that overwhelmed her. Her hands were shaking and her voice was trembling.

"I'm truly sorry. I don't know what got into me."

"Do you remember how you'd bring your random boyfriends over every time dad was on a business trip?" Flora and Betty stared at each other as combats getting ready for a fight. "I would force myself to sleep with headphones locked up on my ears. I remember every time you slapped me for telling you to stop what you were doing. I kept quiet not telling anyone your dirty secrets and when I finally did, you convinced dad to throw me out."

"Oh my God!" Ricky gasped.

Betty cleared her throat. "If there's anything I can do to make up for my mistakes let me know but don't throw me out. I have nowhere to go."

"It's always about you, now you want me to accommodate you because you have nowhere to go. Where are your boyfriends?"

"Flora please...."

"What did you do when I told you that one of your boyfriends tried to rape me?" she wiped tears from her eyes with her free hand. "Let me refresh your memory, you locked me up in the basement and said I was a good for nothing liar." Flora's head began to pound, she threw her palms to the side of her face.

She never understood why her mother did the things she did or why she was so distant with her. Betty had always been unpredictable and Flora never pretended to understand why she was that way. Betty has never been a mother or a wife to Brock, all she ever did was go shopping and watch TV all day. Betty always wore designer clothes, shoes and carried the most expensive handbags. To her, marriage was a convenience and had Flora to please Brock.

"What now?" Angie said, pulling Flora from the past.

"I'm leaving."

"That's not what I meant. I want to know what your decision is regarding the will." Angie folded her arms in front of her chest.

"If you don't contest the will then we can move fairly quickly." Paul looked at Flora. "Do you plan to challenge the will?"

"Why? You made it clear that my father's provision to me was to take it or leave it deal."

"That's correct." Paul nodded.

Flora should have known that her father would leave for her everything under conditions and still control her from the grave. Now suddenly, the lines were blur and she didn't know what to think anymore.

"Can I sell off everything?"

"As soon as they legally belong to you."

Thirty million dollars in exchange for her pain. After that, she could go anywhere she liked.

That night Flora had a dream that turned into a nightmare. She dreamed she'd finally fulfilled her father's will and was able to leave Westfield. She was a free woman buzzing with pleasure. The sun heat and poured all over her, heating and bathing her in the light she could hardly see. She was finally warm and wearing a killer dress. Life couldn't get any much better.

Ricky was in her dream. He handed her a bag full of cash like she had won a lottery. She shoved it in the co driver's seat of her Ferrari and jumped in. with the ten million beside her, she headed out of town feeling like a celebrity, and the closer she drove to the Westfield city limits, the lighter she felt.

She drove to the city limits for what seemed like days, and when freedom was just miles away, her Ferrari turned into a robot car, leaving her on the side of the road with her bag of cash. She stared at her car and continued to walk towards the city limits.

The LEAVING WESTFIELD sign remained barely visible no matter how long or how fast she walked. She started to run, frustrated at the same time. She leaned to one side to counterbalance the weight of her bag. The bag became too heavy but she kept on going. Her sides ached and she couldn't run any further. The city limit was still in the distance. She knew for sure that she was still stuck in Westfield forever. She was sweating now as she opened her eyes.

She sat up in the bed. A silent scream on her lips. Her breathing was choppy and she was sweaty. It was the worst nightmare of her life. She wondered why Ricky was the only person in her dream and the money. Where did it come from?

Chapter 3

The next week was boring for Flora. She stayed in her room most of the time and avoided everyone especially her mom and Angie. She walked to the living room and curled up on the plush leather sofa. She had a novel on her hands, while listening to music from the background.

Ricky walked in totally yummy in a pair of blue jeans and adidas sweater. She stared at him then back to her book. She had to admit that he looked good, she just hoped the sensual hunger did not show up on her face.

"Hi, you eating in tonight?"

He dropped his earphones on the table. "I thought we could both eat out tonight."

"I wish I could, I have other plans," she said honestly. "I have to finish this book and the other one." She indicated the other book beside her on the sofa.

"You read too much. You need a break."

"No, I don't. You are just spoiled."

"And you are the one who started spoiling me." He moved closer to her, his rich, sweet masculine scent teasing her.

"You don't give up, do you?"

"I don't, especially knowing that you need someone to talk to." He scratched the tip of his nose.

She grinned, her expression flashing from annoyed dominant female to smiling confidence.

"You are lucky I'm in a good mood today."

He plucked her book out of her hand and tossed it to the couch. He grabbed her arm and tugged her up. "I promise that you will enjoy our dinner, I'm new here but spontaneous, you know." She landed with a thud on his hard male chest and gasped moving as far back as his holding would allow. She tried to break it even though he wasn't hurting her in the slightest beat.

"I guess I will tag along." She rolled her eyes. She never bothered to ask about his background, but it didn't take a rocket scientist to know that he is a reserved person.

"Why didn't you ask your sister-in-law to go out with you? Just asking."

"I wanted to go out with you."

"All right. Please tell me we won't stay long."

"Your wish is my command." He sealed his promise with a kiss. On her cheek, slightly next to her lips. The sane part of her brain told her that was a kind gesture from him. She'd always been adept at avoiding any talks or handshakes between them. Her body had different ideas, the eyes that had only seen one guy before him went instantly blurry.

Some small part of her sanity asked her what she thought she was doing. A deeper voice, that of love, told her she would never get a chance like this one. Her heart and mind demanded compatibility to that distant voice. "Shall we?" Ricky whispered.

Ricky drove his humming, masculine mid-life crisis old junk to the Cozy Hotel. The dusty 1955-1963 Mercedes Benz 300sl gullwing pulled up into the parking lot of Cozy Hotel. It was half past eight. Most of the lights on the neon sign was still visible, hadn't burned out which means it was a middle-class hotel.

Though physically and mentally exhausted, Flora still managed to find some humor as she walked in. she never waited for Ricky to pull out a chair for her. She was used to doing things on her own.

"You look relaxed today," Ricky said. He gazed around, his eyes stopping at her seriously held bun.

"I have good and worst days in case you haven't noticed." She stopped and stared at the waiter who was waiting for their order.

"I'll have burger and fries." She pointed at the menu.

"I'll have the same," Ricky concluded.

"You had to copy my order." She rattled out to fill the silence.

"I've realized that you are more down to earth, you can let loose and enjoy the different flavors of life. I was expecting you to order steak maybe, you know what they say about steak on a first date."

"What do they say?" she chuckled a little.

"They say, if you want to impress a man, order stake on the first date. It's insanely sexy when a lady knows how to cut her steak, as long as you don't jab it with your fork, hack it with a knife and certainly don't swallow a five-inch piece of meat. It drives men crazy, makes us think of you taking control in the bedroom."

"Good to know, too bad we are not out on a date." She raised her eyebrows at him and pushed a stray hair off her face.

"That's what you think." He smiled at her then, his intense gaze never leaving her face. She was doomed. He looked even yummier when he smiled.

"I am...." She tried to speak but could not find words. "You...." She cleared her throat, looked around the hotel for anyone eavesdropping, the hanging flowers, the wind chimes tinkling over their table. He was waiting for a response. She turned and looked at him, her kneecaps felt like they were cracking then she froze.

Her body prickled with pure mortification. She never wanted to continue blubbing because her acute embarrassment was causing a hot flash. She hated the sweat fests as she called them whenever she was nervous.

"Let's talk about you now. What's your full names?" She tried to avoid his staring. She noticed the alarm on his face. "That question froze you like a constipated animal."

Ricky stared at her, his eyes almost twinkling out of his head with humor as she waited for an answer. He still paused for an imaginary drum roll.

"Ricky O'Donnell." He wanted to lie but couldn't.

"That's a good name. I don't know why you hesitated." She saw the corner of his mouth twitch. He was trying not to smile.

"It has occurred to me that you had quite an interesting childhood." He stopped as the waiter placed their orders on the table.

"I'm sure you're good at a lot of things, reading other people's minds." She drawled, then snapped that traitorous mouth shut. "I mean I'm sure you have many talents apart from health and fitness."

Darn. Must escape from Mr. Gorgeous, she thought.

"I'd really like to help. If you want anyone to talk to anyone, you know where to find me." His voice was soft and manly, it would taste so good hearing it close to her ears. "It's against my princely nature to let a damsel in distress to fend for herself or fight her own demons."

His gaze raked her face, devoured her features like he was seeing her for the first time. His face was chiseled, every edge sharp. His lips compressed, jaw set. His eyelids were too low for her to see his eyes, he was studying her. His gaze lingered in her jaw then he looked into her eyes.

He held her gaze for a long moment, hazel to hazel. Tense beyond bearing, her nerves stretched tight. She wanted to compose herself. She was not going to let him know she fancied him.

"This damsel is one tough cookie and does not need a man in her life to help her get rid of her demons. If I want a horse, I can damn well buy myself the whole stable."

"I like your sense of humor. I knew you had it in you. I'm already fascinated by you. You are definitely not a damsel in distress at all. Maybe you should ride on this charging horse. You won't regret it."

She got air stuck in her lungs. She figured it was her past drowning her, she felt something hard on her chest. It was her instincts pushing her to jump on him.

"You should forgive your mum, everyone makes mistakes." His brows rose but his expression didn't waver.

She leaned her forehead on her palm and banged it a few times.

"Again with that topic?"

"It's okay if you don't want to talk about it."

"Mr. O'Donnell, you are a pain in the butt." She smiled.

He nodded amicably, "Been called worse, I like it." He spoke while laughing like a drunk hyena. He leaned in and whispered in her ears, "This is the best night of my life."

She closed her eyes. He was more attractive close up.

"Is this how you lie to all women?" she asked, strangled.

"No, I only feel this way because of you." *Would it be inappropriate for me to tell him that he smelled nice, or inappropriate for me to deeply inhale his smell and make a moaning sound?* She wondered.

"What do you mean?"

"You are not what I expected." He laughed. She could almost feel the laughter in her. "I think"- he stared into her eyes, "I think it's you, this new humorous you."

"This does not sound good, not at all." He sat back on his seat which was good because she was feeling dizzy. She could never say she believed in love but she did believe in lust. Too bad, the object of her lust was soon to be related to Angie, her worst enemy. She inhaled deeply like a drowning rat.

"I don't know, I don't know," Angie said as she put her hands over her ears. "I've told you that we are working on it." She told the person on the other end of the phone.

"We haven't heard from you or Ricky," the man said.

"Everything is fine, everything is going according to plan. We will send you the money soon." There was a knock on the door. "I have to go." Angie said before hanging up.

Betty walked in the room with a smile on her face.

"Am I interrupting something?"

"No, I was just talking to my boyfriend. Apparently he couldn't make it. That's why he sent his brother. He can't even support me when I'm down."

Angie was a great liar and Betty bought her lies all the time. Betty always loved her more than Flora. Angie kept her secrets and never judged her.

Angie screamed, long and piercing. She jumped up and down indulging her temper and usual tantrums. She punched the air and stomped around. She held her head up and screamed through a clenched teeth. When she grabbed her cell phone to throw it across the room, Betty made a lunge and grabbed it from her.

"Angie, this is damn expensive."

"I can't get rid of this pain in my heart, he keeps giving me excuses why he couldn't come to the funeral." She fought Betty for the phone. "I hate him, I hate him." She screamed again.

Betty wrestled the phone from her hands. They ended up in the heap on the floor huffing and panting.

"Want an ice scream?" Betty asked.

She screamed through clenched teeth.

Chapter 4

"That can't happen again, Flora. It's okay if you don't want to go out with me," Ricky said to Flora the next day, he tried to keep a smile off his face.

She pulled her sweater close to her body. It was mid-morning, she tried not to react to his comment.

"Uh..." she said. "Am I supposed to thank you for not wanting to take me out again?"

"I don't want any gratitude. I don't want to make you feel uncomfortable."

What will Ricky do if she ripped her clothes open and wriggled naked body like a flamingo in front of him. She thought. No, too much desperation but still, the image made her smile. When Ricky saw that smile he murmured "Damn," he stepped into her room, slung an arm around her waist, pulled her closer and then kissed her.

His jaw tightened and she was leaning on him, she said softly in his ears. "Thanks for not kissing me and not wanting to go out with me." He rolled his eyes at the sarcasm in her voice. She laughed so loud, he wanted her but she wanted to hide from everyone. All she could think of was what Ricky would look like naked on her duvet. Delicious!

He kissed her again, harder this time. She wanted him to stop even as she kissed him back. Even as her tongue encouraged him. Even as she wound her arm around her neck and clung to him. He slid his hands down her sides, then slipped his fingers beneath the loose edge of her sweater.

She felt his fingers lightly caress the small of her back. His warm palms slipped to her abdomen fanning lightly to her heated flesh. The knot in her stomach tightened as the sensations tingled her chest.

"I have to go now," he whispered. There was an awkward silence between them.

"So Jerome called me yesterday." Angie smiled at Ricky over the rim of her coffee mug. "Won't it be lovely for you to call him back?"

"Lovely?" Ricky agreed enthusiastically. The last thing he needed was to call or hear from Jerome. It was the only bad thing in an otherwise bleak prospect.

He had contemplated creating some excuse to get out of a situation like this but it was too late. Ricky felt the tension between them like an electric filament ready to burn at the touch of a switch.

"You have to talk to him. He wants the money or we die," Angie said.

"I'm not talking to him or going through with your plans." He flicked a glance at Angie's unsmiling face. The least he could have done was call him back. She thought crossly.

"Where the hell did that come from?"

"I'm done with this kind of game. I have a feeling that something bad is going to happen." She pulled her chair far enough to look at his face.

"You can't back down on this. We had an agreement. I suspected my uncle would leave his stupid daughter all his money that's why you had to tag along."

"I'm not stealing from her or anyone in her family. I think we are going too far with this," he replied although he doubted she would agree with him.

"Don't you think you are taking your boyfriend role too seriously? I saw you two leave the other day," she questioned in a low tone.

"I just want to do the right thing."

"The right thing? You are my boyfriend and she is an assignment."

"This game is dangerous and I want out." He licked his lips and shifted his gaze to the left. "She is way too smart to fall in your trap."

"Are you interested in her?"

"I'm not, I only want to do the right thing. If I were you, I'd try and do the same."

"You sound crazy, I can't believe you want to do the right thing when our lives depend on this. What did she tell you to make you change your mind?"

"Nothing."

"Then I guess we'll both have to lose. Do you think she would want to date you if she knew who you truly are?"

"Is that a threat?"

"No, I'm trying to warn you that you will never get away with this either way." She sipped her coffee.

"That's why I can't go through with what you want."

"I will have to sell you out."

"You don't have to. I'll be leaving soon."

Flora had no choice - it was a direct order from her old self. Never fall in love she stood on the porch, key in her hand. When she came back for the burial, falling in love was not on the list. She inserted the key into the lock but didn't turn it. She surveyed the front porch, she stared at the flowerpot dangling on top of her head. Then she lifted her gaze to the nearest neighbor and beyond.

Hopefully, the neighbors were all asleep or dining in a local café. She didn't want anyone spying on her.

She and her old-time friend had pulled an all-nighter, first in a local bar until they were tossed out at three then on her way home with a bottle of vodka. They had passed the bottle back and forth, she wanted to rest. The door opened before she could turn the knob. It was Ricky.

"Great! Just what I needed," she muttered.

"What are you doing up so late?" She was barely audible. She sank into the chair on the front porch as Ricky walked close to her after slamming the door. He was not happy.

"Are you okay?"

"Yeah, I'm fine." He sounded gloomy. "I want to tell you that I'll be leaving soon." Her lifeless fingers started shaking. She stood up, her anger rising. She did not exactly appreciate being left alone, after she told her friend how she was falling in love with Ricky.

"You lied to me," she yelled at him. He could smell the alcohol from her breath. "I don't know anything about you, all I know is that you will be related to that evil Angie soon."

"What was I supposed to say?" He put his palms up in the air, exasperated. "You don't want to talk about yourself either."

"Yeah, Ricky, I thought there was a damn good probability that you would hear everything from your sister-in-law. I was also hoping, hoping against hope that you wouldn't want to know. That you would love me for who I am today."

"I would never let details slide, especially details about the woman I'm starting to have feelings for."

She stared at him and tears filled her eyes. She never expected to hear that from him. His eyes flashed with all his pent-up pain; she knew he felt something for her.

He stood two feet from her, she could smell his-mint, aftershave and his cologne. "I know you don't feel the same way and I get it. You have a cruel past and don't trust anyone."

She swallowed hard. Hearing what he said made butterflies erupt in her stomach, fluttering about as her heart raced. He put his hands on his hips pushing his jacket back. She wanted to scream, show him how much she loved him. She had never opened up to anyone like she did to him. All she wanted was to give it a try.

"All I ever wanted was to change my names. I remember when I left home, I spent much of my time in the car thinking up new names. I wanted a new identity, a new life. Covering up my old life was my priority. I even told people I was from a poor family and my mother was a housekeeper."

"I'm sorry." He groaned.

She knew what was coming, and she braced herself for a nauseous cascade of painful memories. "Child services were called to our house several times. I went to the hospital on a number of occasions and would lie about my mother hitting me whenever she was drunk.

"You are the strongest person I know," he said.

She felt hot tears swim to her eyes. "Want to know more? My mother told my father and the doctors that I was mentally ill. I doubt the doctors believed her but my father always believed her. I denied being mentally ill but it put me in an emotional tailspin."

"I can't believe your biological mother would do this." He was furious and she could tell the anger was directed to her mother. "I still can't believe you lived through that."

"Me too." When she remembered that time, she didn't know how she survived it. "I once got courage and left but my mother hired a private investigator who brought me back. Every time my dad would not give her money to spend on her boyfriends, she physically took her anger out on me.

"That's outrageous." Ricky breathed.

"She always convinced me that my father will never believe me because he knew I had nowhere to go, nowhere I could think of. She was trapped."

"And what did your father do to you?" His voice was low and pained.

"You mean apart from listening to my mother and neglecting me? He always evoked fear in me, even though he always said he loved me no matter my mental condition. Ricky was pale, his face tightly drawn.

"Come to me, babe." He pulled her into his arms, hugging her close, swung her up, into the house and gently placed her on the couch. Her head was spinning and she was sobering up. Sad stories followed each other as if she had written a line up.

"I'm so angry with your mother right now. I feel like I was the one neglected and mistreated. I haven't felt like this in a long time."

"I didn't want to tell you about my past. I hate when people feel pity for me."

"I don't pity you, on the contrary, I respect you. But damn, I'm furious about what you had to go through. I want to go to your mom's room and tear her apart. I'm sorry you had to go through that."

"It's okay," she said trying to make light of it. "It's done. I have a new life. So please help me not to punch your mother on the face the next time I see her. She is a sick woman, Flora, no sane mother would ever do that."

In her mind, she realized now that it was her parents' issues, not hers. She remembered the kid she was, how unbearably hurt she was. He stroked her back, his cheek next to hers. And she clung to him. She lifted her head up and at some point, he was crying. Huge and masculine man wiped tears from his eyes.

"I don't want to see you cry." She also started to cry. A man who cried for what she went through! A man who cared so much about her to cry in the first place! She saw light, golden, bright light through his gesture.

Her warm wet lips found his, he kissed her back, pulled away and kissed her back. She knew he was fighting it. She should have pulled away to make it easier for him. She would

have to give up all her inheritance before she would give up the
next hour of her life. They gave in to the rush of passion. Her
hands went around his neck, he picked her up and they were on
her bed.

Chapter 5

Flora spent almost an hour in a piled-up haze, styling her hair, applying her make up for the first time, squeezing herself into a red dress. The ten minutes she spent wrestling herself into her spanx weren't terrible. She was not a fashion victim nor was she a fashion bystander.

She couldn't tell between Dolce & Gabbana and Ralph Lauren but she felt hot and sexy. She didn't know what their little designer signatures were and didn't care because she felt those who cared were clueless. And because they reminded her of her mother.

"It's a fashion statement." Her friends would tell her. The reason why she maintained her friends for so long was because they share similar tastes in books, music and creating things. Her friends are good with fashion, with her it's ad campaigns. Her world is media and PR. People think it's crazy but fashion, glamor, and adverts are somehow connected.

"You look beautiful." Her mother said as she came down the stairs, while Flora narrowed her eyes. She carried a pair of Jimmy Choo, one of the surviving pair she promised not to wear.

"Thank you." Her mother never expected that kind of polite response from her. She looked like a new person.

"You look exquisite," Ricky murmured breathlessly as he approached her. Angie's eyes and cheeks flashed red.

"What's the big occasion?" Angie asked, her lower lip quivered. Flora kissed Ricky on the lips and answered with a smile.

"Nothing special," she answered. Before Angie's pique could swell into a full-blown tantrum, she brushed a kiss on her forehead and sat down on the couch. She finally felt like she was winning.

"You can use my car if you want," Betty offered, looking at Ricky.

"Great, mom," she replied. "Any gas in it? You think that flashing E means you're doing an excellent job, don't you?"

"Haha, funny," Betty replied.

Flora was enjoying her new carefree attitude. She had been dreaming about that moment for over twenty years, being sexy and successful, dating, looking Angie in the eyes and saying "Haha I won."

"I will apologize until you forgive me, honey. I'm truly sorry."

"Uhh, another thing you like saying. Seems to be another theme in your life." Ricky smiled at her sarcasm.

"People make mistakes," Angie said, focusing on Ricky. "That's why pencils have erasers."

Her voice was cold, so detached. Flora thought a glacier had launched itself from the North Pole between her and Angie. Something made her furious, she didn't know what it was and was more than happy to find out.

Angie felt sick with pain and loss, she could tell. She watched as Angie gripped her stomach. For the first time, she felt liberated. Whatever it was that provoked Angie made her smile. *Was it my dressing?* she asked herself.

"Let's go my love." Ricky said.

Angie gripped the staring wheel until her knuckles turned white.

I don't belong here. I hate this town. I hate everything about it. I can't wait to leave. Her words still echoed in her head.

She wanted to grab Flora and shake her but she had to hold still until her plan work.

"I hate her," she muttered. She leaned her head back and stared up. Her phone buzzed and she picked it up. It was a message from Jerome.

I'm in town, meet me at the town mall.

She started the ignition and headed straight to the mall.

Jerome was always punctual. Angie saw him standing next to an ATM machine in a hoodie.

"Tell me you have my money." He held her by the arm.

Angie's scowl matched Jerome's. "Go to hell."

A slow smile started at the corners of Jerome's mouth, then he burst into laughter.

"What did you just say?"

Angie didn't see the humor. "Goddam it, I will get you the money," she swore.

Jerome sniffed and scratched the side of his neck. "The amount has gone up."

"Now I get the real reason you are here. Money. You don't care about what we owe you as long as you get to develop an empire."

"Sure why not? I admit that this is a gold mine. I want it so bad the thought of it keeps me up at night just thinking of all those million-dollar houses and ways to spend all that money I stand to get from you and your clueless cousin."

"You think you have a chance with her?" Angie slowly put her hand on his shoulder. "I think you better leave before you make things worse."

Jerome crossed his arms over his chest, not looking like he planned to leave anytime soon.

"That's another issue. This town. Look at it."

"Yeah."

"Look around. You are all alone. How sure are you that Ricky hasn't turned his back on you? we all know how greedy he can get. You are one person, Angie. I have an army. I will take it the easy or the hard way. Whichever way is successful."

"What's your point?"

"You get me my money and a share of the jackpot cash."

A warm sweat dampened the back of Angie's polka dotted blouse and she froze on the spot. She stared at a short man in a brightly colored shirt and an impatient woman who'd been checking her phone every five seconds for the last thirty minutes.

The woman made a disapproving sound, indicating that she was done waiting. The woman pushed her way past them as she turned back to look at Jerome.

"I'm not sharing any money with you. I will pay what I owe you and that's it."

"Well...." She shut him out before he could finish talking. He was wrong. She wasn't going to share her money or her boyfriend with anyone. Because she had a plan. She wouldn't make a fool of herself if she stuck to the plan. It was foolproof. She hoped. She had already successfully carried out the first part of it. At least that's what she thought. There was no need to doubt herself or Ricky about the rest. Besides, it was too late to back out now. She thought.

"I will keep you posted."

"You are in no position to make demands. You two work for me, don't forget you owe me."

It's never too late.

The words from her mother rang her mind. It was one of the many clichés she liked using on a daily basis.

But in this case, they were true. It wasn't too late for her to take everything away from her cousin. She could still walk away with everything without causing any damage. Whatever problems that arose from her action could be fixed. She could always find a way to explain them.

She handed an envelope to Jerome.

"This is the first payment. It is half of what I owe you. You will receive the other half and we are done."

"We are not done until I say so. And tell Ricky what I just told you. Oh, and let him know that I will chop off his favorite part of the body."

"We'll see about that." She walked quickly to her car. She had to admit that she was scared. Jerome was not a man to argue with, it was always his way. He was a man who believed in torturing his victims psychologically and emotionally. His words rang on her mind.

The boat was no yacht. Hell no, it was a beat-up old fishing boat that Ricky rented. To Flora's eyes, it was an exact duplicate of boats in Game of thrones.

"I bet the fishermen caught a lot of fish in this baby," she said. If only she knew where Ricky was taking her, she wouldn't have worn her sexy red dress, and the Jimmy choo felt uncomfortable. She now realized why she never wore them. "I can also smell one of them," she added. She smiled back when Ricky gave her a cold warning.

When they reached the cabin, Ricky pulled the rope tighter and helped her out. She stared at the beautiful sky.

"This is amazing. When did you plan all this?" she asked, a smile written all over her face.

"You deserve so much more."

Upon closer inspection, there was a five-foot-wide path meandering through the forest but leaves covered the walkway.

The further they walked to the cabin, the more run down. The place wasn't exactly Disney land but she loved the ambience. The sounds of the chirping birds filled her ears.

Cupping her hands, she looked inside the window of the cabin. There was an old fashion juice bar with stools covered in worn red plastic. She rubbed the dust from the glass and looked closer. She couldn't believe she was spending the night with Ricky in this cabin. There were bird photos, plastic birds and bird posters. She turned away for a moment and leaned against the door of the cabin. Ricky opened the door.

"I need to shower first before I do anything," she said as she looked around for the bathroom.

While Flora showered, Ricky threw together a sandwich. He was pensive.

He thought of a way to tell Flora about who he truly was. Now he had to figure out what to do next. He kept staring at his phone and ignoring Angie's calls. He had to tell her the whole truth and come clean. It was time.

Sandwich in hand, he went outside and stood on the front porch to eat. The view gave him pleasure. With the second sandwich devoured, he went back to the house and headed to the closed bathroom door. He didn't hear noises from the shower.

"Are you doing okay down there?"

"You wouldn't happen to have seen a dryer anywhere?"

"No."

"Okay." She opened the door. "I'm sure body lotion is out of the question."

She looked damn hot in his T shirt. Though she was skinny, her curves were so feminine. Her waist was tiny and her butt filled out the T shirt quiet well. Though her hair was still spiky from being wet, she still looked gorgeous.

"Can we elope and go somewhere to start over?" This question shocked her but she was happy to marry a fire fighter.

"Yes," she said without hesitation.

This is what Ricky needed to get out of the messy situation. He was in love. There was no going back.

"You look good," he murmured as he kissed her gently on the mouth.

"Thank you. I actually prefer a simpler look."

"I love you." He stared into her eyes.

She said nothing.

All she could think of was if he was speaking the truth. She never believed or trusted anyone. She kissed him gently on the mouth. For the first time she understood a saying she'd heard as a child *to love is to lose control*.

THE END